Bosco

A Debt Owed Damsel In Distress Dark Mafia Billionaire Romance

Calabresi Mafia
Book 7

L.K. Ryan

For questions and comments about this book, please contact 304 Publishing Company at info@authorlkryan.com. Visit the official website at www.authorlkryan.com

*Readers who keep me motivated, love my crazy characters,
and want more.*

The Calabresi Family Tree

Elio Calabresi: Father, Retired Don
Adelina Calabresi: Mother
Savio Calabresi: Boss
Sante Calabresi: Underboss
Renato Calabresi: Enforcer
Elio III: Consigliere
Vincenzo: CEO of Calabresi Holdings
Giosuè: New York Boss
Bosco: New York Underboss
Armani: Enforcer

Synopsis

Being widowed and kidnapped wasn't part of her life plan...

After losing her husband, Giselle has focused all her time and energy on building her career in the fashion industry. Now her life and her budding career have been thrown into unexpected chaos when she discovers she owes a debt she never knew about.

Bosco isn't above getting rid of witnesses, but something about Giselle made him take her home instead. He's willing to share his body, but not his secrets.

Bosco awakens something in Giselle she had never experienced before. He might seem hard and ruthless, but she's falling for the man behind the façade. When Giselle discovers Bosco's ties to the cartel, she wants nothing more than to escape. The only problem is, she's fallen in love with her captor.

If you enjoy steamy romances, forced proximity, killer,

kidnapping, billionaires rescuing damsels in distress, then you'll love Bosco.

Introduction

Have you signed up for my newsletter?

Join today and find out all the latest in new releases, contests, giveaways, sneak peeks, and more.

www.authorlkryan.com

Disclaimer

Warning: There are a few scenes that may trigger the reader. . Be aware. Contains strong language and explicit sexual content and is only intended for mature readers. A dark mafia billionaire romance with an asshole alpha male, possessive, and aggressive. This story may contain unconventional situations, language, and sexual encounters that may offend some readers. This book is for mature readers (18+).

Chapter One

Giselle

The frustration in our marriage at him putting work before us as a couple really made me look at my husband in a different light. For the past few months, he'd been on phone calls all night or working late, missing dinner—and even our anniversary celebration. We promised to travel the world one day, focusing on growing closer, building a life, and having kids together. Lately, I felt like everything we wanted was falling apart. I hated being in such a weird place with my husband, but he had been distant. Tonight, I planned a dinner, and then a trip for the weekend. I dressed in one of his favorite colors—light blue— and pinned up my hair the way he liked. Everyone recommended that we try Bliss, a restaurant that was well-known for their desserts, and I knew Jason loved anything with chocolate.

Jason worked as an accountant for his father's firm, for major companies. He'd worked for him since graduating college.

He ended his call at last and placed the phone on the

table, giving me his full attention. I rolled my eyes and felt tears coming, which I quickly wiped away before they fell.

"It's supposed to be about us reconnecting tonight, but you always put work before me all the time."

Jason smirked and reached across the table to cup my chin. A tingle shot down my spine. "Giselle, stop worrying so much. I am all yours tonight."

After the waitress had filled our champagne glasses, I gulped it down with a wide smile, leaned forward, and locked our hands together. "Finally, so I was thinking we could—"

Ring!

Here we go again! His phone rang, interrupting us. Jason picked it up with a grimace. Finally, he answered, holding a finger up for me to wait. Seriously? I wanted to toss his phone in the ice bucket.

"This is Jason," he answered.

Annoyed, I picked my purse up, rose from the chair, and stomped away from the table. People watched, and I really didn't care if it embarrassed us.

"Giselle! Get back here."

I flipped him off. "Screw you, Jason." My heart raced as I opened the door. I picked up my pace and grabbed my cell phone to call a cab when I reached the end of the block. Suddenly, I felt a strange flutter in my belly.

A cold chill went down my spine as silence filled the air like something was going to happen.

Pop!

Suddenly a loud shot went off, then I heard a scream and swiveled around.

"Oh my God!" A second piercing scream. A group of people stood together near the restaurant door. People ran in and out of the building for help.

My throat went dry and my pulse raced to see Jason, lying on the ground not moving. I rushed back over to him and grabbed his hand. "Jason! Jason! Call the police." Who would do something so terrible? I looked up as more people ran over. I looked around the area for anyone to help when I saw a man standing near a bike under the light pole, smoking a cigarette. I got the same strange feeling from a few minutes ago, along with a bunched knot in my throat. A brief stare-off between us made me quickly focus back on my husband. Sirens suddenly wailed, and I waved at the EMT to come help my husband as they parked and hopped out with their equipment.

"Hold on Jason, please baby," I begged, gripping his head tightly, and pressed a kiss on his cheek.

"Giselle..." he whispered as his eyes slowly closed.

* * *

"Giselle! Hello, Gigi!" My sister snapped her fingers in my face and pulled me back from the same dark night I find myself daydreaming about that horrible situation for the last four years.

"Sorry, Mallory."

Mallory placed a hand on my shoulder. "Jason again?"

Anytime I heard his name, it put me back in that same dark place I tried to escape on every anniversary of his death. My husband was killed four years ago, and all I wanted was to have him back—even if it meant having to deal with his long work hours. Despite those moments of me being pissed about him missing our dates, I would give anything to have him back.

I pushed a piece of hair behind my ear. "Is it obvious?"

Mallory stopped in front of Angel's Bakery and faced

me. "Have you stopped going to the counselor?" Whenever I had a moment of disappearing in a conversation, she brought up my therapy sessions.

It was a sunny afternoon in Queens, and we wanted to meet for lunch and a snack at the corner bakery.

"Mallory." The tips of my ears grew hot, and my head started to pound as she tried to analyze me.

Her head tilted. "Listen, as your sister I want you to be okay, and you're not, Giselle." The corners of her mouth twisted downward like she felt I would have a meltdown or go crazy.

"I will be." I smiled, giving my best rendition of a lie.

Mallory, being older by four years, took on the role of big sister to the highest degree. If anybody tried to say something or fight me growing up, she would stick up for me. I always wanted to follow her when I was younger, but we formed bonds with different friends in school. She focused on her goal of being a top chef, and I loved being a fashion writer.

She gripped the door handle. "Come on, I have a craving for red velvet cupcakes, and you're paying for them." The warm smell of cinnamon and chocolate filled the air, and the chatter of people laughing reminded me to live again.

We bumped shoulders, laughed, then sauntered into the bakery as my body froze at the familiar weird feeling that something bad was going to happen. My body couldn't move.

Mallory continued to walk forward and turned to face me. "What's wrong?"

"I-I think—"

"Giselle, get down!" Suddenly, Mallory's eyes widened

in shock, and she started screaming. She pointed over my shoulder.

For some weird reason I turned to look out the window and saw two men with guns shooting at each other.

Pop Pop!

The entire bakery ducked down—except I was stuck in place, like it felt when my husband was killed all those years ago. It was as if a stone had dissolved inside me that wouldn't let me move.

Ratttta!

"Fuck!" a man shouted and rushed through the door.

I watched another man throw a bottle into a business across the street, it erupted into flames and took my breath away.

"Get the fuck down!" the same tall man shouted at me and sent more shots back at the guys across the street.

Mallory was my saving grace, taking me by the hand and yanking me to the ground.

"What the hell, Giselle!"

"We need to get out of here." My mind was over-whelmed at my reality.

I motioned to the employee exit down the hall. "The back door."

Another customer ran by us. "Who is that guy?"

"Who cares? We need to get to the police," Mallory fussed while a host of people crawled on the floor toward the back exit.

"Bosco, we got him," explained one man, who looked like he was going to war, wearing a bulletproof vest and all black clothes.

Bosco was the tall man who burst through the door. He wore a leather jacket, and his deep, dark eyes scanned the bakery. He nodded, reached in his pocket, and removed his phone. He had arresting hawklike features and full lips. Trouble was clearly something he was used to; he probably dealt with it daily.

I felt a tap on my arm.

"Sounds like the police are coming," she whispered.

I moved behind the counter, praying they got there quickly. "Thank God." Perspiration formed on my forehead.

"We need to leave, Giosuè just spoke with Savio," he said.

Mallory sighed, starting to stand when the door chimed again, letting us know they left. I slowly stood from the counter and stared at the chaos outside, with the firetrucks, ambulances, and police. For a second, it looked like a battlefield. My sister grabbed my hand, and I followed her to the front as the police came to the door.

"Ma'am, are you alone?" a police officer questioned.

A cloud of smoke filled the air. I covered my mouth with the sleeve of my coat.

"No, a few people are still in the back," I mentioned.

"Come with my partner to answer some questions," the officer explained.

"We didn't really see anything," I expressed, not up to being stuck in a police station all day and night.

Mallory whipped her head around at my statement.

He narrowed his eyes at me, so I must have seemed to be lying to him. He wasn't aware that the same guys who came into the bakery with guns were facing me across the street.

"Sorry, sir, can I talk to my sister for a second?"

"Sure, we'll get your statement last." He closed his notepad and walked back inside.

Mallory grasped me by the shoulder and stood in front

of me. "Honey, I know you've been through a tragedy, but we need to help the police so they can catch the people."

"Actually, we need to go, Mallory."

A casual acceptance of violence had engulfed me ever since Jason died.

She clenched my hand. "What is going on with you right now?" She must have sensed the supercharged tension in me.

"Listen to me, but don't look." I sighed. "The guys that came in with guns are staring at us right now. That's why I told the police we never saw anything. There's something about them staring at us that means it could be our last time talking."

Mallory started to turn, and I pinched her on the arm to face me.

"Okay, we should go."

"I agree."

She slipped her keys out and trekked back to her car. The smell of a burning building drifted in the air. We climbed in and made a U-turn to leave since they blocked off the main lane. I gazed through the rearview mirror and saw the two men, still watching us, as the car drove down the road.

"We were just in a shootout." Mallory relaxed in her seat. Her cheeks grew faintly pink.

Neither of us were hurt, which really made me feel grateful for not pushing to talk with the police. I scrolled on my social media and saw a thread with video and photos of the bakery, then me standing in the middle of the bakery. People were standing outside to record and be nosy. The entire block was filled on each side. Cars honked to get through.

"What the *hell*?"

"What's wrong?"

I shoved my phone in her face. "The bakery is all over social media and news even up in Chicago."

Mallory snatched the phone as she turned at the light to head in the direction of my place. "Let me see."

After Jason's death, I moved out of our two-story home on the Upper East Side and put the money toward a town-house near New Jersey. Downsizing helped ease the burden of maintaining a two-story home. Luckily, I still worked for *Forward* magazine part-time, so income wasn't a problem, and Jason had insurance, so the safety net helped me through the grieving process since I didn't have to worry about bills. His parents never liked me, so when he died, they stopped pretending—especially after they got a divorce—and I did the same thing after his funeral.

Mallory appeared in front my building and parked, turned the car off, and scanned each thread.

"Mom and Dad will lose their minds once they see us in the middle of a shootout."

I shuffled out of the car and upstairs, removed the mail from the box, and unlocked my door to hear the sounds of my dog barking for me.

"Hi, my little prince."

Prince, a small pit bull, wagged his tail and snuggled up to my foot. My therapist told me that having a dog would help keep me busy. At first, I disagreed because being responsible for an animal was like having a child.

I bent down and picked him up and flipped through my mail as I kicked off my shoes.

"I need a drink," Mallory complained and walked toward the kitchen.

Prince wiggled in my arms, and I placed him back on

the floor, watching him head to the corner of the living room.

Mallory came out of the kitchen with a bottle of wine and two glasses. I picked the remote up to turn the TV on and sat back on the couch.

Ding!

"Who could that be?" Mallory wondered.

I raised my hand and stood to answer. "I got it, pop the bottle open, please." I snatched open the wooden door.

"Miss Giselle Ford." It was a younger guy with dark brown hair, wearing a flower-delivery shirt and standing there with a bouquet of white roses.

"Yes." My wariness seemed to grow.

He shoved the flowers at me. "These are for you."

"I never ordered any flowers. Mallory, did you send flowers?"

She came up beside me. "No, why would I order you flowers?"

"I think you have the wrong address."

The guy handed off the paperwork. "Giselle Ford is the name ma'am, please sign here."

I scribbled my name and took the receipt, admiring the pretty dozen roses. "Thank you."

Mallory leaned forward to smell them, taking the card, and I snatched it back.

"Hey, my name is on the card."

"Then hurry up and read it. Are you dating someone?"

I flipped the card back and forth, taking in the sweet citrus scent. "No, all I do is work and come home to Prince." I removed the card and read the words to myself.

You saw nothing.

In cursive, words a veiled threat sparked my anxiety.

"Gigi, hello, Gigi!" Mallory stood in front of me, waving her hand in my face.

I rushed back to locate the driver and looked up and down the street. There was no flower truck outside, just kids playing in the street. Through all my years, I had never been in a fight or gotten yelled at by my parents, but the moment my husband died, everything bad started happening. I whirled around to head back inside when I saw two men wearing all black, lingering next to a light pole. Most people who lived on my block were couples and families, with a few retired people who I helped shop for.

Knowing that someone knew my address and delivered flowers with a message basically threatening me after what happened today scared me. Gangs ran rampant in New York and New Jersey. My sister would probably want me to move in with her or our parents.

I lifted the bouquet, marched to the kitchen, tossed it in the trash, and ripped the note card. Mallory snatched it out of my hand.

"What are you doing?" Mallory stared at the card.

"Mallory, give it back." I snatched it out of her grip.

"Is this what I think it is?" In disbelief, Mallory pulled out a stool and sat on it.

"Yes..." I bit the inside of my cheek to keep my nerves under control.

I stood against the counter, head thrown back, eyes closed in thought. Mallory jumped up and ran to the phone on the wall, I rushed to pull it from her grip.

"What are you doing? We need to call the police!"

I placed the phone back on the hook and raised a hand in the air to calm her down. "Relax, Mallory."

"Giselle, are you seriously letting someone threaten us?"

"We have no clue who sent the delivery, let me research first before we go calling the police."

Mallory dramatically tossed her hands in the air. "Fine, where do you propose we start?"

"The flower shop."

I ran back to the trash can where I tossed them and removed the sticker off the side with the flower shop information and dialed them up.

"Tulips and Berries Flower Shop," the customer rep answered.

"Hi, I received a delivery today of white roses with a note card. Can you tell me who sent the delivery."

"Oh, I remember that order. It was about an hour ago," she responded, chipper.

I brushed my hand across the back of my neck nervously. "Yes, it was sent to me without a name on the card."

"A guy purchased the order over the phone," she replied.

"Did he leave a name?"

"No, sorry."

"Thank you." I sighed and hung the phone up.

Mallory came over to me and stretched her arms around my neck, leaning her head on my shoulder. "Maybe we should call Dad now."

"She said it was a man that made the purchase over the phone."

"Come and stay with me."

I moved out of her hold. "I will be fine." The last thing I wanted was to add a burden on her family.

In response, Mallory stepped back, shook her head, and turned to go to the bathroom.

For the past few weeks, work had increased for me, and

she'd tried to get me more involved in her family dynamics. She wanted me to cut down my work hours and start dating again.

I reached for my glass of wine and opened the fridge to pull out items to start dinner, right as Mallory came from the back holding her phone to her ear. She kissed me on the cheek and waved goodbye.

"Older sisters," I mumbled under my breath.

I pulled the pots and pans out to start on the shepherd's pie and salad, turned the music up on the radio, and continued to drink red wine. Prince popped in, wagged his tail, and moved near his dog bowl to eat.

"Be good, Prince."

Ding!

I dropped the knife, wrung the towel in my hands to clean off the spicy, creamy sauce, sauntered to the door, and pulled the curtain back to see a box on the ground. I slowly twisted the knob, bent down and picked it up, then shut it again.

As soon as I removed the wrapping it popped open and what I saw made me stumble back in shock.

"*Jason*," I whispered to myself.

Chapter Two

Bosco

My father kept the door closed when he was in a meeting, so I often listened in to hear about certain deals and to find out how he ran things since one day, I would work alongside my older brother as an underboss and carry on the family name.

I saw the light linger through the door and heard my name. I peeked in and saw Giosuè and Papa, smoking a cigar in his favorite chair, while the rest of the house slept.

"Bosco almost got into a fight earlier today."

"He's your responsibility."

Giosuè groaned, tossed his head back, and stared at the ceiling.

"He won't listen to me."

Dad rose from chair and moved to sit on the edge of the chair. "Soon you will be in position as the Don, make him listen."

Papa told all three of us that our positions should never overshadow our brotherhood.

"And if he fights me on decisions, then what?"

Dad smirked and hit his knuckle on top of the desk.

"Bosco screws up, but that is why I have you and Armani to clean up after him."

* * *

Armani sat on the right side of me, and Giosuè stood in front of us, annoyed and frowning about the shootout that took place in the territory that we covered. Ever since the deal to transport from our docks and through some of the trucking companies we owned happened, the Don let me handle most tasks, and the news that most of the situation got news coverage had made it to his radar.

Giosuè scratched the side of his cheek. "Bosco, tell me again how half our territory is under watch by the police now." He sighed.

"Armani called me when he went on delivery because some people weren't paying up, I went to handle it and got into a disagreement with Titus Graziano's people."

His furious anger prompted him to toss the chair across the room. "We can't have a war right now." In high stress situations, the adrenaline kicked in and my brother would try and take over everything,

"Then let me take him out."

Giosuè paced back and forth. "No, and I heard it was being broadcast on network television, we finally make it to a good place and something pops off."

Armani and I exchanged glances.

"There's something else."

Giosuè's eyebrows raised; his top lip curved up menacingly. "What?"

"A few witnesses." I knew I bore some responsibility for not killing the people in the bakery. Contacts said a few people spoke with the police.

"Are they dead?" His lips pressed tight.

Armani rubbed his chin. "No."

Giosuè chuckled and sat on the edge of the table. "Let me understand correctly: You were in the middle of a shootout, the news got video from anonymous people, and the police found some witnesses, but you let them live."

"It's complicated." I hated it when he tried to act like I wasn't the underboss who helped build our family business. Being the middle child, I was known as the fuck-up who didn't take anything seriously—except fucking women.

Giosuè slammed his hand on top of the table. "How many fuckups as my underboss should I let you get away with, Bosco?! If you weren't my brother..." He pointed his finger at me.

I jumped out of the chair and glowered at him. "Say it."

He waved me off. "You know what we do to people that can't get the job done."

I leaned forward and removed my jacket. "Fuck you, Giosuè!"

My brother's familiar mask of fury descended once again as he charged at me, and Armani stood in the middle of us to block him with his arm. Giosuè took a step back, the door opened, and his best friend and right-hand man Nero marched inside.

Even though he was my older brother, I would never let another man try to treat me like a little boy. Each of us was a boss in our position, and he would respect me, the same as any other mob boss of a cartel.

"Ah shit... what's the problem?" Nero stared at us. Giosuè scoffed, walked away, removed his phone, and started typing on it.

"The shootout near the bakery," Armani recalled.

Nero peered at me. "That was you?"

"It was not on my to-do list for the day, but when someone tries to kill me, I have no choice."

"We always have a choice," Giosuè grumbled as he ended his texting and pushed the cell back in his pocket.

"Do I need to run interference with the police?" Nero wondered. His expression stilled and grew serious.

"Possibly, I know one of the witnesses."

The entire room went silent at my statement.

"Give it to Nero so we can pay her visit." The contemptuous tone, cold and exact, from my brother reigned over the room.

"I already have some men on her location watching."

Instinctively on guard, I hated when we butted heads on situations, Armani as the baby of the family, along with our sister, handled Giosuè's mood swings with ease.

"Send word to take her out." Giosuè's demeanor switched from anger to confusion within seconds.

I pinched the bridge of my nose, hoping to keep him calm. "Unfortunately, this will not be an easy task."

"What are you not telling me, Bosco?" Giosuè narrowed his brows.

"She works at a high-profile magazine, it could hurt things for us."

Nero whistled, and Giosuè chuckled, balling his fists, ready to punch me in the face. It would be like him to make it seem like a bigger problem than it really was. Armani and I never brought up how he'd stalked and kidnapped his wife, then caused a war with multiple enemies. We backed him up without question.

"Right now, the best play is keeping her under surveillance."

"Nero, run a background report on her." Giosuè seethed and gave me a hostile glare.

Unless I took a deep breath and calmed down, my anger would cause me to kill my brother, and then Armani would jump in the middle. He was usually on my side, and Nero, as usual, would have Giosuè's back. A full-on fight between brothers would make our parents roll over in their graves, and then Uncle Elio would call a family meeting. There were too many cousins in our family to fight head-to-head with my big brother—the Don of the family.

I sat forward to meet him with direct eye contact. "I am the underboss. I can do the background check."

"Nero's job is to handle things to make sure no mistakes happen," Giosuè countered.

"Time out, this pissing contest can happen another day, we need to be figuring out the Graziano situation," Armani said.

"Armani's right." Nero slouched down in the chair.

"The Graziano family wants to pick up more land without permission," Giosuè mentioned.

"Which caused the shootout, his men tried to go in and take payments from businesses for protection," I explained.

"What do the other families think about him pushing up on prime real estate?" Nero investigated, swinging his head around to look at each of us.

I shrugged and scratched the bottom of my chin. "Not sure. I planned to meet with a few of them later today—of course, if my brother gives me permission." I smirked.

Giosuè flipped me off. "Do it discreetly and find out if any other businesses had any interruptions. Making a move will hurt us more than anyone," Giosuè replied.

"I agree," Nero said.

Armani clapped a hand on my shoulder. "See, you boys do think a lot like," Armani joked.

"What else is happening?" Giosuè stood with his hands in his pockets.

"Some clients want to increase their shipment, so let me know if we should reach out or keep it steady."

"You run that, I trust you will control distribution at the trucking business."

"On my list of duties, boss." I winked at Giosuè.

Nero and Armani laughed and rose, and all four of us continued to joke around as we left the warehouse. Armani hopped in his car, I jumped on my bike, and Nero and Giosuè climbed in the back of the limo. I slipped on my helmet and black leather gloves, revved the engine, and kicked the stand to head out with them trailing behind. Back on the main road, we all separated in different directions.

While sitting at a light near Central Park, I felt my phone vibrate. I pulled it out of my pocket and saw that one of our clients at a strip club had texted and was ready to meet. At the same time, the men I had on the woman from the bakery were leaving her home.

Honk

The light just changed to green and the car behind me continued to honk annoyingly, so I turned the bike off in the middle of the street, let the stand down, and hopped off. I stalked to the expensive Mercedes Benz and busted the window with my elbow, reached through the window, snatched the keys out of the ignition, and threw them across the road.

"Honk again, motherfucker," I warned him and waited for him to try me.

"You're crazy!" he shouted.

I tapped myself on the cheek with a grin. "I know."

I jumped back on my bike and drove away as other cars

honked at him. The Calabresi temper ran in everybody and not coming down from the argument with my brother pissed me to a higher level.

* * *

Fifteen minutes later, I finally arrived at the club and parked in front, where I knew my men could watch in case anything funny happened. I lifted my helmet, left it on the bar, and pointed with my chin at the bartender to send my usual drink to the booth.

"Bosco! Good to see you." Allen's voice echoed with underlying mischievousness.

"Sit Allen, we are not friends."

He laughed and sat back in the booth. "I ordered a drink to celebrate," he said, then rubbed his hands together.

"We haven't agreed to your deal, Allen."

Allen furrowed his brows in agitation. "Come on, Bosco, you and I both know money would be great if you upped our shipment."

I gripped the edge of the table. "It is not about the money."

He pursed his lips and chugged the alcohol. "Since when do you not like making money?" Allen pulled back to lean against the couch.

Money moved Allen more than anything. He was known for getting people caught up with the police. At first, I was hesitant to agree on the initial deal, but the product moved faster whenever we sold off guns. A few times, he wanted a few of our drug connections, but I was picky when it came to the drug game. Our family name being linked to anything beyond oil, art, and gun trade came at a high cost.

Slowly, I looked around at the other people in the club. "It's a bigger risk if we take in more. Extra security, paying off more police. Allen, you live in a fantasyland."

He relaxed, sticking his hand in his jacket, removing a cigar from his pocket, and lighting it. It was a non-smoking club. "Think about what we could accomplish."

"Look, I can't agree until I speak with my brother."

"You used to be the wild one, not waiting for permission from Daddy." Allen chuckled.

Typically, if someone showed me any type of disrespect —especially about my family—then I'd blow his entire face off, but I had to play nice. Over the last few months, Giosuè had gotten on me for killing people because of my temper.

"Allen, I suggest you correct yourself. Like you say, I used to be wild. Disrespect me again and find out how wild I can get." I pushed my jacket to the side and showed my gun, then eased out of the booth and stood.

"We're not done!" Allen yelled.

Out of pettiness, I reached for his cigar and dumped it in the glass he was drinking from. "I will be in touch when I feel like it."

* * *

I showed up at the address of the woman who witnessed the shooting. Before we take out any loose ends pertaining to her, I'd like to have Armani research any problems.

I arranged to have flowers dropped off at her place with a message so that she'd know we could get to her at any time. Keith and Mikell had been with me as guards for over ten years, and I trusted them like they were family.

I tapped on the window. Keith rolled it down, and we shook hands.

I scanned up and down the street. "When did she leave for work?"

"About an hour ago?"

"Anyone come in and out?"

Keith handed his phone to me and showed me some pictures. "Just the other woman who was with her."

"Put someone on the other woman as backup if we need to force her hand."

"You sure we shouldn't take them both out before they can do any damage?" Mikell suggested.

I sighed and ran a hand down the back of my neck. "No, if they had only witnessed Graziano's people I wouldn't care, but they saw us."

"How did it go with Allen?" Keith inquired, took his phone back, and stuffed it in the cupholder.

"He wants more product. Look into him for me. I'm not gung-ho about pushing too fast."

Keith nodded and started up his car.

I glanced at the front of the magazine office she worked at and saw her laughing with a group of people while walking down the street.

Mikell craned his neck, removing his seatbelt. "She's on the move."

"Stay here I got it."

"We should be with you, boss!" Keith called out.

"I can handle a little trip down the block. I will call if I need back up."

"Big Boss won't like us leaving you alone." Keith drove out a harsh sigh.

"Who's going to tell him?" I winked, jogged across the street, and followed closely behind the group of three women and one man. They stepped inside a restaurant that was fairly busy, which gave me cover. I snuck in behind them and listened to them talk with the hostess before grab-bing a table.

"The videos we saw online showed your picture, are you sure you're okay, Giselle," her friend explained.

Giselle.

Giselle raised her hand and cut her friend off. "Already talked to the police and they promised to keep me updated."

Her statement gave me pause.

"Scary to be out at a place where you would never think a shootout happens."

"My sister is worried enough for the both of us," Giselle said and handed her menu back to the waitress.

"Well, I am excited to be working on the new spread for the fashion show," said the red-haired girl.

"Anything else for you?" The bartender approached me again.

"No."

An hour later the group stood and started to leave out of the restaurant after paying. I stalked toward her at the door and bumped into her by accident and one of her friends caught her by the wrist before she fell.

"Hey, excuse you!" the guy yelled. I turned to face them. We made eye contact, and she froze.

I smirked.

Giselle swiftly turned and grabbed her friend by the shoulder to keep them from walking up to me. I headed back to my bike and drove back to her place. Keith and Mikell stepped out of the car. I marched up her steps and glanced around before I popped the lock and walked inside.

"Check upstairs," I explained, stepping into the living room, looking around, and taking in her soft scent as it wafted in the air. It was obvious a woman lived there; it was decorated in light colors, with long white curtains, and a widescreen TV mounted on the wall. I came across the answering machine on the table and a pile of unopened mail. Nothing seemed out of the ordinary—mostly bills and food magazines. I gazed at a few pictures on the wall and paused in shock.

"Fuck."

Keith trekked into the living room. "All clear upstairs."

"I bugged the phone upstairs. Wait isn't that—" Mikell came around the corner.

"Jason Ford," I muttered, staring at pictures of her and Jason at their wedding.

A few years ago, we got word that Jason dipped into company funds and worked with a few of our enemies. Giosuè put me in charge of making him disappear, and I took it personally that someone we trusted was going behind our backs. I never met his wife, but we knew he was married. His father tried to come at me about his son's death but knew we'd put him down as well.

Mikell stalked over to the window, peering behind the curtain. "Giosuè's going to be pissed."

I chewed on the corner of my bottom lip. "We can't make a move yet, she's too exposed."

"Shit," Keith mumbled.

I jabbed a finger toward the light on the side table. "Put a camera in here, kitchen, and hallway."

"How long will we keep her under watch?" Keith pressed.

* * *

Four Years Ago

Nero stalked into the bar and dropped down in a chair. He pushed his phone toward the middle of the table. Armani and I looked down and watched as he got sent to a voice recording.

Nero clasped his hands together, cocking his head to the side. "Listen." Nero gave a clipped nod at the static recording.

"Bosco and his family will never know we worked together, and it's perfect."

There was a familiar voice that was hard to identify.

"I want the route, so I can get men ready to take everything they have. Get me the information," Steele demanded as a loud slam came through the phone.

"Steele."

Nero clicked the red button to end the recording. "Steele and Jason Ford. You wondered who robbed the trucks over the past six months." Nero scrolled to another text and pressed play on a video clip.

Steele and his men—along with Allen—held one of our workers hostage, then killed him when he refused and took the truck with our product in it.

I paid for his funeral and sent his family money to cover their costs for the year.

"Find him and bring him to me."

* * *

I was jolted out of my daze by Mikell snapping his fingers. "Not until I can snatch her up without causing a public panic."

Keith and Mikell started to put things into place. I reached for the photo on the table and stared at Giselle's perfectly pouted lips, soft brown eyes, and sharp arched brows. Finally, my men finished and backed out of her place. Keith followed behind my bike as I headed home. I arrived in less than thirty minutes to my nearby condo in the city, then laid my helmet and jacket on the couch. The light rain hit against my windows that overlooked the city. I turned on the heat and flicked on the light in the kitchen to grab a beer. My sister decorated before she moved back to Italy. She came to visit at least once a year and stayed at this place. Often, I forgot I had the place—unless I was too tired to drive home.

I reached into my pocket to pull my phone out and dialed my brothers on three-way calling.

"Why am I hearing Allen talking about moving to another supplier?" Giosuè inquired.

"He's faking to try to get me to agree to his demand of more product."

"Should I pay him a visit?" Armani quizzed.

"No, I can handle Allen."

"Seems like you're handling too much, Bosco."

Respect came automatically from me to my older brother, who was the Don of our cartel. Knowing that he would continue to pick at me when we both knew he was really mad at something else beyond his control only made me want to kick his ass.

"Fuck you, Giosuè."

"Save that for the bitch you have coming to your place," he hissed.

Armani chuckled low, and I wanted to bust him in the mouth for laughing at Giosuè's comment.

I yawned and stretched my head from side to side. "You have no idea what I have going on. Worry about your own family."

The memory of Giselle's full oval face, plump breasts, and wide hips etched in my mind again.

"Bosco as my little brother I will give you a pass once."

"Aye! Stop it. We are brothers," Armani grunted through the phone.

I took a deep breath and closed my eyes to control my temper. "Armani's right, I apologize."

The grumble from my stomach prompted me to rise from the couch, walk to the kitchen, and take out the left-over meatloaf from the other night. Ready to eat, I placed the call on speaker, then applied slices of bread from the top counter to put together a sandwich.

"Allen will be fine. What news do you have, Bosco?" Armani probed.

I was still not ready for bed. I walked into the office and sat in a chair. "We might have a problem."

"What?" Armani wondered.

I logged in and checked emails, then brought up records about Jason Ford. "Giselle."

"The girl that saw you?"

On Jason, I scanned the last known communication between Armani and me. "Yeah."

"What are you not telling us?"

"Giselle Ford."

The quick look at each other at the restaurant brought back that night.

"Ford, why do I remember that name?" Armani muttered, snapping his fingers together in thought.

"Who is that?" Giosuè inquired.

"Jason Ford's widow."

Silence filled the line, and it meant that Giosuè was ready to kill anyone who had connections to Jason Ford.

I remembered those sad cries when she saw her husband lose his breath. She didn't necessarily know it was at my hands. I only stuck around for a few seconds to make sure that the body was taken by our clean-up team. The police never made a big fuss—even though his father was well-known in the business sector. I had him watched, and the mayor made it go away fast—for a price.

"Tomorrow, I have a flight out of the country to spend time with my wife. Make sure you handle *Giselle*, and nothing comes back on us, Bosco," Giosuè snidely remarked.

"Already my plan." I disconnected the call, dropped the phone on top of the desk, and glared at the wedding photo of Giselle and Jason in a major newspaper.

With a long day behind me, I stretched and left the office to finish dinner, take a long shower, and go to bed so that I could wake up early and find a way to put Giselle Ford where her husband resided.

Chapter Three

Giselle

Today's weather brought out comfort cooking, and I wanted to make vegetable soup, cornbread, salad, and cheesecake for dessert. My mom continued to talk about gathering a group of her church friends for a girls' brunch in a few months and wanted me to help organize it. I promised to set some time aside to help with plans once work slowed down. Sometimes, Mom could be impatient and expected us to drop everything and focus on her.

I finished cutting the celery. My hands would not stop shaking from seeing that familiar man the other day. He had the same dark, soulless eyes as he did at the bakery when I begged my coworkers to leave the interaction alone and insisted that I didn't know him.

Her fingers molded the graham cracker crust in the bowl for the dessert topping. "Honey, what do you think about the gift bags?"

I grabbed the oven mitt from the counter, bent down, opened the stove, and removed the cornbread, then put it on top of the island. "It's a good idea."

She turned around and cleaned her hands on the towel that was slung over her shoulder. "Are you all right? Sick or something?"

"Huh?"

"You are quiet today." A mom's natural instinct is to worry about her child.

"Tired from work, I have a lot of stuff to write up for the fashion show."

Mom pushed off the counter, whipped around, and started mixing the ingredients in the pot.

"Something more is going on."

I stuck my finger in the cheesecake mix for a quick taste. "How are you and Dad going to celebrate your anniversary? Mallory wanted to get you guys a vacation weekend at a bed and breakfast."

"Trying to change the subject."

I hid a quick swallow at her knowing my intentions and turned away. I gently bumped her by the shoulder and wrapped an arm around her waist. "Can you keep a secret?"

Mom reared back. "From your father?"

I slumped, biting my lip and hanging my head on her shoulder. "You know Dad is going to start into his protective mode."

"He's your father, Giselle," she chastised.

"Mom, please." I felt like I had to keep quiet and avoid spilling any details about the bakery.

After Jason's death and going through depression, my parents wanted me to live back at home to keep an eye on me like I was a little kid again.

Mallory appeared, wearing a raincoat and holding an umbrella. "It's coming down so much out there."

"Leave your wet coat at the entrance, Mallory," Mom said and waved off my sister's kiss.

Mallory paused and stuck her tongue out behind her back, then walked back to the living room. Our parents raised us in a household where we felt protected and open to talking with them about any concerns, but sometimes we wanted to rebel since our father was a cop. Dad spoiled us and catered to our mom, showing us how we should be treated by a man.

"Now back to you. Tell me," Mom insisted.

I took after my mom with being curious and nosy on subjects that revealed something deeper, which is why I went into journalism.

"The bakery shooting." I hoped she could understand my dilemma.

Mom stopped stirring. "What about the shooting?"

"You know I was one of the people there."

"Yeah, and you spoke with the police, right?"

Mallory came back into the kitchen, grabbed a glass from the cupboard, turned on the faucet for water, and joined us to spy.

I felt a migraine brewing, so I opened the cupboard to get some Advil. "I talked to them but really never answered a lot of their questions."

"Why not?"

"Well...I kind of received a message." I shifted uneasily, not sure how to answer.

"A message." Mom paused for a moment, as if hesitant about saying her next thought.

Mallory placed her cup on the table, and disappointment covered her face. "What are you talking about, Gigi?"

"The note from the flowers said not to speak." I wished I could be anywhere in the world instead of having a conversation that might put my family in harm's way.

"What? Why am I hearing about it now?" Mallory fussed, then sat back in her chair with a frown on her face.

"Wait a minute. Are you talking about a threat of some kind?" Mom probed, then looked between Mallory and me.

"I was there at the bakery and never received flowers."

Mallory and my mom felt like I needed someone to fight my battles when I was growing up since a few girls tried to bully me. Unless I was around my sister, I mostly kept to myself in school or stayed in the library. As a thirty-year-old woman living on my own, I still had to handle their feelings with kid gloves and not push them away.

Dad rounded the corner, dragged my mom into a hug and kiss, tapped Mallory on the head playfully, and kissed me on the cheek.

"Dinner ready yet? I'm starving. Mallory I will take your car to get the tires replaced," Dad spoke, pulling a chair out for himself.

"Thanks, Dad," Mallory responded.

My heart was beating at a dizzying pace.

Mom moved out of his arms, took the pot from the cupboard, and set the food up to eat. One of her favorite gifts from Dad was a 72-piece dish and pot set that she'd gotten for her birthday. "Gigi, go ahead and tell us."

"Later, we should eat."

"Maybe Dad can get some answers," Mallory suggested, refilling her water.

Dad peered at me. "Answers?"

Mom, Mallory, and I kept our mouths shut.

Dad dropped his elbows on the table, staring at me. "Talk." Since he was a retired police officer, we grew up understanding when he would go into a cop mindset.

"No, I'm fine, Dad." I sighed. "Mom raved about your anniversary gift."

Dad hated it when we kept him out of specific conversations. Mom passed the basket of cornbread to me. I took a piece and dipped it into my soup.

Mallory covered her mouth with her hand and coughed. "She's lying."

I rolled my eyes at her. "Shut up." I sat back in the chair annoyed. Mallory and boundaries never mixed together.

"Gigi, be nice to your sister she's worried about you," Mom insisted, then stood from the table, trekked to the fridge, grabbed whipped cream for the dessert, and sat back down. "Honey, I am having the girls help with planning our anniversary, nothing more."

"Probably going to cost me a lot of money," he grunted, then chuckled at Mom's frown that cascaded down on the entire table.

"Dad with us no longer living at home, Mom wants you two to spend more time together. I mean besides golfing," I instigated.

"She loves golfing."

Knock Knock

Mom dropped her spoon and stood, but Mallory waved her off. "Who could that be?" Mom lifted her napkin to wipe her mouth, then pushed her cell to my dad to show off the pictures of the bed and breakfast.

Mallory swiveled around in her chair and ambled to the front door. "I got it. Finish eating." A few seconds went by, and Mallory came back to the kitchen holding an envelope and flowers that matched the same ones I received at home.

My sister lifted the flowers to her nose. "Look what came. Dad I know we rag on you, but did you get Mom flowers?"

Mom clapped her hands in excitement, then reached

over with both hands to capture him by both cheeks to press her lips to his. "Honey, you got me flowers?"

"Maura, you know I was never a flower guy."

"Mom, can I see the card?" A weight seemed to press against my chest, robbing me of breath. He'd found my family.

My annoyed older sister slapped my hand down. "Shouldn't she read the card first? I mean, it was delivered to her." Mallory scoffed, then sat back down.

I reached over the table to grab the card out of the flowers before she could read anything. "Mallory, eat your food." It was the same handwriting that I saw when I opened the envelope at my house. I tore open the card as big knots formed in my stomach.

Nice to see you again.

My family was not paying attention. I glanced at them, laughing and talking about the flowers, then I slipped the card in my pocket, continued to eat, and joined in the conversation.

* * *

After lunch with my family the other day, I made sure to destroy the note before any more questions came up. Once traffic picked up, and I reached my destination, I climbed out of the cab wrapped in my favorite cream-colored trench coat. Regrettably, the expensive boots I wore were too tight and thin around the ankle, so they hurt my feet.

The barista at my favorite coffee bar called out my usual order. I thanked them and trekked to the office elevator. The heated building warmed my body and gave me a jolt of energy.

One of the other writers handed over a few magazines.

"Hey Giselle, I have some mail that came to my desk." Colleen and I started around the same time over five years ago.

I sat down and removed my coat, sipping on my mocha latte. "Thanks, Colleen."

Colleen stood in front of her cubicle. "You are so welcome. Are you excited the fashion show is coming soon?"

"Already planned my outfits for each day."

"We are having some parties, you should come."

"Ugh, Colleen, you know parties are not my thing," I groaned, flipping through a magazine on my desk.

Colleen wrote for the lifestyle section at *Blue Magazine*. She helped run the online section and wanted me to hop on board, but I liked sticking to print because I only had to work a few days a week. From what she told me, her hours could be from forty-sixty a week, depending on whether a high-profile client was scheduled for both departments.

After Jason's death, Colleen was new to the city, and I was starting over. I got to know her, and she was like a little sister who I could talk to when I needed real advice.

"Think about it, Giselle: You are only thirty," she griped, plopping down in her chair. "I know a few celebrities will be at the party—and word is Armani Calabresi is coming."

"Who?"

Colleen looked around and scooted closer in her chair and whispered, "Armani allegedly is a billionaire and single."

I marked up my column, scanning over any mistakes. "I am not interested in dating."

"I hear he's extremely toxic and rich, you don't want to

miss out on that combination." Colleen laughed and rolled back over to her workstation.

"Meeting!" the editor yelled, sauntering down the hall to the conference room. I grabbed my coffee and phone, then followed the crowd.

One of the other assistants held the door open for us, and I slipped in and sat. Colleen poured coffee into her cup near the coffee cart. Andrea, the editor-in-chief, stood at the front of the table next to the whiteboard.

"I am happy to relay the momentum for the fashion show coming up is making a lot of people happy." A smile lit up Andrea's face.

Her assistants passed around a printout of the logistics sheet.

"What you have received is a full agenda, so everyone from the biggest names in music, Hollywood, and even a few political figures, will come for *Blue Magazine*'s annual fashion show."

"Any return on interviews for the night?" I asked.

"Interviews won't be granted that night, but I have a few feelers out."

I pulled up my story base to type all the notes in my computer. A few people raised their hands giving pushback on some of the plans that would cause us a long night when paparazzi blocked traffic in and out.

Andrea strolled to the whiteboard and cleaned off the list of items we discussed as the team started to leave.

I hopped up from my seat, pushed my chair back, gathered my things, and whipped around to follow Colleen.

"Giselle, can you give me a moment?" Andrea requested.

I waved at Colleen to keep going. "Sure."

Andrea clapped her hands. "I heard about the bakery

shooting. It was all over the news. Then I saw a shot of you in the background with the police."

I sighed, not wanting to relive those moments again. "Unfortunately, it was the wrong place and time for cinnamon rolls." I laughed it off.

She chuckled along and sat on the edge of the desk. "Do you need time off? I want to make sure your mental health is good. It looked terrifying."

"I'm fine, Andrea."

"Okay, I have to double check, you have a lot of work coming up and it can be demanding."

"Honestly, work is what I need to distract me."

"All right, well, keep me updated if you change your mind."

"Thanks, will do."

Andrea walked alongside me out of the room and back to her office, with her assistant on her trail. I checked the time on my watch, listening to my stomach grumbling. Colleen would suggest going to lunch as a group, but after the last time, I felt like being alone to run through story ideas since I hadn't done any work over the past few days, and I had a deadline to meet on Monday.

Ben stuck his arm in his jacket, prepared to leave. "Colleen and I are going to lunch, you want to join us?"

Colleen shut down her computer and picked up her purse.

He stood in front of me. "I hear the dumpling place around the corner is great," Ben said.

I logged out of email on my iPad, shoved my notes in the cabinet, and lifted my purse and coat.

"Actually, I have some work for a deadline coming up," I mentioned and ambled to the elevator. "Have fun."

"Which means she's going to the park to eat and work, so boring," Colleen jested.

The elevator doors dinged open. We stepped on, and Ben pressed the lobby button. Laughter filled the small space. We arrived at the main floor. More people stepped on after letting us move out. Sun beamed down on me. I covered my eyes with the palm of my hand, then sauntered to the sandwich and smoothie shop across the street. I stood in line, waiting to give my order. I felt my phone vibrate and took it out of my purse to see my sister's texts about my parents' trip.

Mallory: *I found a place.*

Me: *Send me how much I owe on the package.*

Mallory: *Mom's going to love it, and Dad gets to fish.*

Me: *He's going to drive Mom crazy. Lol!*

I peered up when the cashier called for the next person and gave my order, then stepped to the right side near the counter to wait.

"Number Five is ready," the cashier stated.

I picked up my order and sat at the booth in the back, unfolded the chicken wrap, sat my purse and device on the table and started to put my fashion article together. Suddenly, a voice cleared. I scanned the man standing at the edge of the table up to his eyes.

"Can I help you?" I peered around the shop and prayed someone would help if I screamed.

"Giselle Ford?"

"Uhm, I-I-" I stammered, rubbing my sweaty hands together in fear.

He raised a hand to cut me off. "My daughter is a fan of your work."

I gulped down the water, then set the glass on the table. "Thank you." I smiled and felt relieved.

He pointed toward the window. "Excuse my manners. Do you see that blue tinted town car outside?"

I nodded. "Yes."

"Here's the thing: Your husband owed a debt to my boss."

"Wait—my husband?" All the blood drained from my face. Would he kill me in front of everyone?

How did he find me?

Was the daughter comment a lie?

The guy removed a picture from his jacket. "Yeah, Jason Ford, right?"

I looked at the picture. My eyes bulged, and I felt myself start to hyperventilate. "My husband died four years ago."

"Unfortunately, he made some enemies, and I have no choice but to bring you to my boss."

"What is your name?"

He wiggled his finger in my face. "It doesn't work that way, and I am trying to be cool, so I suggest you quietly get up before I shut the entire place down."

"Do you really have a daughter? I mean, how did you find me?!" I panicked, glaring at the tall man who had to be over 6'3". He had a menacing look, a shaved head, and light brown eyes.

He planted both hands on the table, leaned forward, and grinned.

"Who is your boss?" I threw out question after question to buy time, trying to reach for my phone to call my sister.

"The bakery shooting brought your face front and center. I can bring in your entire family, or just you." He gripped the back of the chair. "Get up slowly and don't make a scene."

I lingered on him for a moment, glanced at the staff

talking to customers and laughing while I sat here as a complete stranger threatened my life.

I slowly closed my eyes, removed my hand from the phone, and said a prayer. Jason's death was a sore spot, but I thought I had been able to move forward.

I gathered up my coat, iPad, and purse, then started to move around the table to leave when I finally got the courage to shove him back and took off running through the front door as people yelled around me.

"Oh, my God!" a woman screamed.

"Call the police!" I shouted, sprinting in my heels down the block. A few people stopped and stared at me like I was putting on an art show or faking it. I made it to the middle of the street. A few cars honked their horns and cursed at me. Then suddenly, a tight grip on my hair caused me to stop running.

"Shut the fuck up or be ready to die," the raspy voice commanded. I smelled the same cologne I remembered from the bakery, and it stilled my movements.

"Boss she took off fast." He bent over out of breath.

Their top boss shoved me into the other guys. "Take her to the car."

It was broad daylight, and no one in New York thought it was strange that I was being held against my will and threatened in the middle of the street.

"Please wait!" I struggled to get out of his arms. I kicked and screamed.

My job was just two doors away, and I saw Colleen and Ben laughing. In spite of my attempts to get their attention, his team covered my mouth and pushed me into the back of the same car as the one that had been used at the bakery.

Would my family know I was kidnapped?

Thirty years on the planet, and the only trouble I ever

dealt with was a parking ticket that my father helped me get out of when I was seventeen. He wanted me to learn a lesson about speeding.

Hopefully, Colleen or Ben had seen something, or someone on the street would come forward and save me.

It was as if I was in a dream. As a strange smell filled my nose, my eyes dropped low, and darkness surrounded me as I slouched in the seat and fell asleep.

Chapter Four

Bosco

"**A**s the search continues in questions about the latest cartel shootings in the city, our news station will keep you updated. I'm Pamela Winters at KNBX channel eight," the local news reporter explained.

I changed the channel and stood in front of the fireplace, waiting for them to show more recordings from the fiasco at the diner. She was supposed to be brought in discreetly, but Giselle tried to escape. I had watched the entire thing happen from my bike, and it pissed me off. Savio and Giosuè both contacted me and wanted a meeting because of the reckless move.

I listened as the locks turned on her front door. Keith carried Giselle inside and lay her on the couch. So that she wouldn't fight us, I'd ordered a small dose of chloroform to put her to sleep until I could figure out a solution to my problems. Keith stood back, and I pointed with my chin at the door.

"I can handle it from here."

* * *

A few years ago, another robbery occurred at Calabresi Trucking.

I signed off on the load, and my team placed the crates on the back of the rig. Russell, one of my drivers, picked up his outline for the week and climbed into the seat.

"Stay on top of the speed limits, Russell. We can't have any more tickets coming through because you got happy-go-lucky."

"Come on, boss, that was once or twice."

"In one month, and don't make me put up a rule to keep the wives off the routes."

He grinned and thought it was funny, but on long drives he had his wife come out with him. I understood not wanting to be away for long, but they couldn't keep the speeding tickets limited.

Bartlett tapped the back of the truck—it was ready to go —and he drove off.

I stood and watched as the truck drove away from our distribution company. I whipped around and handed off the itinerary and headed back to my office. For the past six years my company got robbed, a few people were beat badly and ended up in the hospital which made me start to put tracking devices on the trucks along with cameras.

"Mr. Calabresi, we just got word from Russell a car is driving really close and suspiciously next to him," my secretary informed me.

I kicked the trash can next to the water cooler, snatched my phone from my pocket, and dialed Armani.

"Get the inventory list, call our lawyer to tell him to head to the spot and he better get there before me." I jogged downstairs and hopped on my bike. "We just got hit again."

"Send me the location," Armani replied.

"Sending it now and let Nero know it's time to lock in on Jason Ford."

* * *

I was pulled back from the memory of Jason's fuckups. Keith pat the hip that showed his gun. "Are you sure, boss?"

"Cover the door, make sure no one comes by."

"Yes, sir." Keith never faulted me on my decisions, but I knew today was too messy.

Giselle stirred from her sleep, cupped her forehead, and muttered under her breath, still not fully alert. A muscle flexed angrily in her jaw.

Normally, a beautiful woman like her would receive a warm, irresistible welcome, but under these circumstances, I had a goal to make her pay for her husband's betrayal. So, I sat on the loveseat opposite the couch and watched her eyes flutter open in confusion.

Something flashed in her eyes.

"You gave me no choice."

She slowly pulled her legs up and scooted to the corner of the couch frightened. "Who are you?"

"Someone that doesn't like to be ignored." I sat forward then planted both hands on my knees.

She clenched her forehead to make sense of what was going on. "You're the guy from the bakery."

"A few of my business associates feel you are a liability."

Giselle froze at my comment; a tremor touched her lips. "I-I-I didn't say anything to the police," she stammered. Her eyes circled around her living room, probably trying to find an escape, like I wouldn't be able to find her again.

"There's no way to leave," I assured her. It was the

weekend, and a few of my guys wanted to party it up to celebrate one of our boys getting engaged. Keith was assigned to be her bodyguard moving forward, and Mikell would be her driver. Even if she felt like he was wrong to take her against her will, it was ultimately my decision.

"I won't say anything. I can give you money. I have about $10,000 saved."

"And your sister? How about your mom and dad." I smirked, lifted from the chair, marched to the fireplace, and grabbed a picture frame of her family. "I hear they're going on a trip next month for their anniversary," I added with mock severity in my voice.

Her eyes widened at my comment. "My family is not involved. Please." Giselle's voice was fragile and shaking.

I slammed the picture on the ground, then stalked toward her to close the distance. "Jason Ford."

"What?"

"Your husband, Jason Ford," I repeated with contempt, wrapping my hand around her neck, tempted to squeeze. Whatever sweet scent she carried pissed me off; it was distracting, so I stepped back to put space between us. Her soft features might have caught other men in a trance, but I would never fall into her trap.

She blinked rapidly and jumped to reach for the phone on the table to the right of her. I lunged and snatched it away, ripping it out of the wall socket.

"You killed Jason," she whispered and rubbed her neck, swaying back and forth.

"Stay here until I can figure out what I'm going to do with you."

"I have work. My family will start to wonder where I am."

"Too bad."

She clenched her fists, gnawed on the corner of her lip.

I slipped my gun from behind me and pointed at her head. "Sit down," I growled.

Giselle raised her hands in the air. "Please, you have to believe me, Jason would never do anything illegal." Tears slowly found their way down her cheeks.

"He owed a debt and never paid up, so his death was ordered by me. Now you are here to continue as payment."

My family would want her killed and it could be done, but I remembered her from that night and thought of a better idea for her to pay back on her husband's debt.

Giselle slouched down on the couch and shook her head. "Jason kept me out of his business, he was an accountant."

"One that liked to skim off the top and rob my business to help my enemies."

A look of tired sadness passed over her features. Giselle wiped her tears away. "What about his family? Shouldn't you go to them for the money?"

"Jason didn't just take money, he took product." I watched her face change from confusion to shock. "Millions of dollars are a lot to collect on. His family is on my radar, no worries."

Giselle's face flashed with anger. Quickly, she tried to dart around the opposite direction of the couch, and I shot a few feet away that caused her to freeze up.

Silence grew tight with tension.

I cocked my head to the side and put the safety back on my gun. "Tsk, tsk, little one."

"My father is a cop," she answered in a rush of words, like it could hurt me.

Our family had a long-standing agreement; the police never scared me.

"A retired cop, one my family has met in the past."

Giselle's head jerked back in surprise, and she linked her hands together. "Are you saying my father owes you money?"

"No, but ask him about the Calabresi cartel." No longer interested in the conversation, I turned to leave.

Keith marched in and held eye contact. I motioned to her and explained that she was to stay there until I said she could leave.

"How long?"

"Until I can figure out how she can be useful to my business."

"She's like a big celebrity, or writes about them, you don't think her people will come asking questions?"

I arched a brow at Keith doing his research on Giselle. "Call me if she tries to leave, or guests come over." I pulled my shades from my pocket and covered my eyes. "After I talk with Giosuè and Savio about how to proceed, I will have some ideas."

I jogged downstairs, jumped on my bike, pulled on my helmet, and drove away from her place. It may have been a little too much to mention that her husband owed our family money, then tell her that we knew her father.

Armani had dealings with him and explained that he used to gamble at our cousin's casino and ended up covering a few jobs for us when we had a few things tangled up with the police.

The blocked street on the left-hand side was causing traffic. I eased through and got to the cigar bar I owned in the nick of time. I parked my bike in the back entrance of the employee lounge. A few members of my crew nodded in acknowledgement. I trekked through the hall and upstairs to my office door, seeing it ajar. I laid a hand on my gun and pushed the door open slowly to see Armani, Savio, and Giosuè watching the security monitors. A storm of applause erupted downstairs, which meant my employees had another drinking contest going on.

I knocked Armani's feet from my desk. "Get your ass out of my seat."

Armani balled his fist up, pretended to box, got up, and moved to the chair on the right of me.

"Mostly we've gotten along in the business by being discreet," Savio expressed.

I raised a brow at his statement because nothing he or my brother had ever done was discreet.

"A second video of you and your people in the middle of the street causing a problem for the cartel!" Giosuè argued, a look of scorn flashed across his face.

The two of them sat at my desk. I pointed between them. "You two are the last people to give any type of argument about being discreet." I slouched in my chair, tossed my keys on the top of the desk, and laid my helmet down.

Honestly, the joke would write itself if either of them believed that I would somehow put a target on our family's name when the two biggest clown princes put our name in lights.

"The only reason we got the video removed is because of our tech team. Your face and Keith's would have been on the Most Wanted list," Savio explained, sliding out of the chair and standing near the bar.

A part of me wanted to get lost in a new pussy instead of my brother and older cousin trying to lecture me on my responsibilities as underboss.

I pressed the top of my mouse and maneuvered to another camera screen. "She's home with Keith. I have her under lock and key."

Savio leaned against the door for a moment. "What do you plan on doing to get the problem to go away?" He tipped the glass and came to sit back down in the chair.

"Her husband stole over $10 million—plus product—with Steele Graziano. We got back two and took his life."

The low whistle from Armani was a sign he wanted blood.

"Plus, her father-in-law is under the impression that she's behind his death."

Savio had no clue about that little secret.

"Why are we just now hearing about it from you, Bosco?" Savio investigated.

"Jason's father only blames Giselle because the family never wanted him to marry her in the first place. I can tie him into the money theft."

Armani passed a glass of Duce to me.

"On Allen, I still think we should pass on his deal."

"Allen called me, and he proposed we get seventy percent," Giosuè exclaimed.

I glared in his direction, hating we looked so much alike. Our mother dressed us up so much that people thought my brother and I were twins. Eventually I looked at my big brother as a father figure after we lost both parents.

"Still not sure about Allen, we get any wrong eyes on our business from him, then I have to slit his throat."

Savio lifted his glass and gulped down the rest of his drink. "We all agree, but seventy percent with an increase in product coming from Italy and Europe will make us a lot of money."

Giosuè scoffed and tossed both hands in the air. "Armani was put in charge as the enforcer, you as my underboss. Can I trust you to even make decisions that will protect the family?"

"Fuck you Giosuè!"

"Giosuè is right, Bosco." A pained look marred my little brother's face. It seemed like he was done being my best friend.

I swiveled my head around to face him.

Armani raised his hand to stop me before I spoke. "I agree with Bosco that everything pertaining to Jason was handled correctly." Armani always played it safe when we fought. "His direction to take him out that night played fair but reckless."

Giosuè and Savio listened intently, while all eyes faced me.

"How do you want to handle everything?" Giosuè asked and raised himself to his feet with a loud grunt that betrayed his age.

"Get the rest of the money, she has to know if he has some accounts under his name or his father's company, then kill him and anyone else."

"All right, we will let you oversee her as your new project—but remember, she's not to be one of your little playthings. Too much comes with her last name," Giosuè reminded me.

I pushed the chair back, hopped out, moved to the window, and flicked open the shades to gaze down at the business. "She's not my type."

I was ready to move on from the conversation. As billionaires, yes, we could ignore the debt since we killed him, but it was about the principle of taking from us.

"Say we move forward with Allen, I will agree to up the amount of product, as long as I get to kill him if he backstabs us."

"Allen is one of our long-time clients, Bosco." The

words tumbled from Giosuè's lips. He sprang from his seat and stood next to me.

I waved my brother off.

"You of all people tell me to keep feelings out of business, we know he's worked with Steele and Jason."

The door squeaked open. One of my waitstaff lightly tapped on the door, gazing at us. "Sorry, sir, I need you to sign off on the inventory," she exclaimed, holding a clipboard in her hands.

My family waited as I read over the document, signed off, and reminded her to never interrupt me again.

"Thank you, sir." Sage winked at me, twisted out of the room.

Giosuè sucked his teeth. "You might be right. If you end up taking him out, then you better have a replacement. Too much product going out, and nothing coming back in to counter it."

"I can bring in more of our crew to back you up," Savio suggested.

"Keep them on standby." I swaggered to the door. My family trailed along, and we enjoyed a few drinks and put a lid on the Giselle situation for now.

* * *

Eventually, the day got away from me, and my head hurt from dealing with nonstop bullshit. I arrived at my main home and looked at the police report from the bakery's shooting. I read the article, saw a few pictures of me, but what really had me sitting forward with agitation on my face was a picture of Steele Graziano—the nephew and longtime rival that I thought was in jail—and Jason Ford's father standing in the back of the crowd talking.

I reached to pick up the landline phone and dialed Nero. "He's out." I zoomed in on the screen.

"Speak to me, B."

I could admit I felt weighed down by the pressures of conformity and being the son of a legendary cartel Don.

"Why am I seeing a picture of Steele Graziano? Someone that's supposed to be in jail."

"He's out of jail?" Nero questioned.

Night drew down like a black cowl. I gripped the gold pen my father received from our grandfather. Each of us had a special piece passed down from Italy.

"Obviously, someone played us because he was there with Corbin Ford."

"Shit, I need to call our contacts," Nero grimaced.

"Immediately. And let them know the money is no longer coming if were getting half ass information," I spat.

"Calm down, your brother told me about the fight earlier," Nero said with unwelcome frankness.

"Do you think he's right?"

"About you being underboss?"

"Tell the truth Nero, I know he's your best friend and all."

"Giosuè is the Don of the family, but he knows I will never blindly agree with him. I told him he was too rough and that you've handled worse situations."

"Thanks."

"No problem. Let me look into Steele, and I will get back to you."

"We're going to let Allen have more product, and if Steele is out, I can guarantee he will be sniffing around our trucks."

"I will get more security on the warehouses and docks."

"Cool, get back to me asap, I know Savio will send more backup."

"The trucking company should have increased security," Nero suggested.

"Already had it on my radar."

We hung up at the same time. I stretched my arms out, stood, and swaggered out of my office and down to the kitchen. I popped open the fridge and pulled out the leftovers, grabbing a fork and sitting at the counter.

She's probably sleeping.

I glanced at the time on the microwave to see that it was going on 9 PM. I got up and tossed the food in the trash, then swiped my coat and helmet and marched out of my place to check on Giselle.

"Keith would have told me if she went missing."

There was light traffic, and I made it to the condo in record time. I jogged upstairs, cocked my chin at Keith, and unlocked her door. The TV was blasting.

She turned to look at me as she was eating from a plate of food that smelled good.

"We need to talk."

By the roll of her eyes, I guessed she was still pissed at me for keeping her under lock and key. Giselle removed the comforter from her shoulders and shuffled to the kitchen in only a sports bra and shorts.

I felt a weird emotion stir through my body, and I stared at her wide hips in the small shorts. "Where's the rest of your clothes?"

"Excuse you." Her mind was spinning with bewilderment at my harsh tone.

"Did my guys see you in that?" The thought tore at my insides.

Giselle scanned down at herself. "What are you talking about?"

The night we first met, I only saw her from afar, and the silhouette of her body was never really shown. In front of me now, her clothes hugged her curves. She didn't have a completely flat stomach, but I'd never cared about women who were extremely fit. Currently, Giselle was giving my men a show. *Maybe Giosuè is right, and she's a complication that we should dispose of immediately.* From my research, she had lost a lot of weight and fallen into a depression after Jason was killed. I shook my thoughts from my head as I took in her bright eyes and full lips, frowning at me.

She's the enemy, I said to myself.

Giselle snapped a finger in my face, one hand on her hip. "Hello, are you listening?"

I clenched my fists. A fiery attitude was something Giosuè got from his wife, and he loved it, but a woman would never run me. I slapped her hand down and walked around her to look in the pot on the stove. An entire display was laid out: green beans, cornbread, meatloaf, and dumplings.

Giselle reached to grab the plate from my hand. "What are you doing!"

I picked up another plate, then a fork, and filled it up with a little of everything. "Making myself a plate."

"That's not for you." The color drained from her face.

What if she poisoned it to throw me off? I thought and then chuckled.

"Enough to feed a football team," I lied, between me and Keith, we'd wipe it all up.

Giselle chewed on her lower lip and stole a look at me. "So! You should ask before taking things."

"You are right—but seeing as though you owe me millions of dollars, I can start by collecting food tonight."

"I don't owe you shit!" The embarrassment quickly turned to annoyance.

I ignored her, shifted around her, then grabbed a bottle of water from the fridge and sat back down on the couch.

Giselle stood with her mouth hanging open at my actions. "Mr. Whoever-You-Are."

I bowed my head and pressed my hands together in quick prayer. "Bosco."

"Bosco, I will call the police if you don't leave."

I eased my hand behind me to remove my gun and placed it on top of the table. "You sure you want to do that, Giselle?"

"Yes!" The misery of being confined was like a steel weight.

"Aaron, Mallory, and Maura would be disappointed if you made that choice."

Her shoulders deflated when I brought up her family. She slumped down in the chair opposite me. "The only money I have is about $10,000 I have saved up. Whatever business you had with my husband has nothing to do with me."

"But your father-in-law has some of my money."

"Okay, then harass and kidnap him," she sassed, then tore herself away with a choking cry.

I grinned and wiped my hand on a napkin. "Your nose scrunches up when you're upset."

Giselle might think it's a game, but she had to hop on board, or she would find herself on the wrong side of my gun.

"Here's the deal, you will get close to your ex in-law to

find out where the rest of my money is, and to find out why he's hanging with Steele Graziano."

Keith eased back inside and looked from me to Giselle. "Boss, you wanted to know when security was put in place at the warehouse?"

Giselle tensed and got up from the chair. I frowned at the way she was showing off her body.

"Where are you going?" I ignored Keith's statement.

"To bed." She sniffed, wiping tears from her eyes.

"We aren't done, go put on some clothes."

Through our stare-off, I could see Keith's head whipping back and forth from the corner of my eye.

Giselle stomped down the hall.

Keith smirked.

I could feel the vein in my forehead swell at him mocking me.

"Stay outside unless I tell you to come in."

"No problem, boss, but I've never seen you jealous before."

"Focus on securing the outside like I pay you to do."

"She's not Italian, you okay with that?"

"I never noticed and don't care."

Giselle walked back in the living room with a long sleeve shirt and pajama pants. "Happy now?"

"Sit, please."

Keith laughed and strode back outside.

Giselle lifted the remote and turned on the TV to avoid any more conversation. I liked it better that way. After tonight, I needed to figure out a better solution for communication because I was bound to strangle her ass if she pissed me off.

Once I finished the food and explained that I would be

back, I slung my helmet into my hand and headed out of her place, leaving the door open behind me.

Chapter Five

Giselle

I removed the rolls from the oven and picked up my glass of wine. I smiled at the beef stew, steamed veggies, and salad, with strawberry cinnamon rolls for dessert. I placed my glass back down, lifted the pot of stew, walked into our dining room, and laid it down. Jason loved my beef stew. We had plans to finally spend more time together and travel. He'd been stressed about money because some of his clients worried when the stock market fluctuated.

I shuffled down the hall to his office and hesitated before knocking. There was loud yelling from inside.

"I told you, it needed to happen later, too many and they get suspicious."

Suddenly, it became silent, and I pushed the door open slowly.

"I sent you the address of the next truck going out." Jason glanced at me and held a hand up to wait. He stayed in his office for long periods of time, and all his college and high school trophies sat on his shelf. When we moved here, I decorated his office and man cave in black and off-white, with his name etched on the door.

I stood in front of him and pointed to my watch. "Jason, dinner is ready." The anger I held a few days ago of him being a workaholic and not taking me seriously crept up again.

Jason stuck his hand out and captured the back of my palm to bring to his lips. "I will be right there." He pecked me on the lips. "No, I'm talking to my wife. Just be ready and I will meet you at Calabresi trucking." Jason hung up, dragged me to his lap, and nuzzled his face in my neck.

I adjusted in his lap to face him and crossed my leg. "What was that call about?"

"Nothing for you to worry about." Jason pinched me on the cheek.

I stroked his forehead, noticing that he was serious and dedicated. "Jason, you look stressed."

"It's just business. We're good." He sat back, sighed.

"Fine, come and eat dinner."

Jason walked next to me to the dining room. "I smell stew."

After he sat in the chair, I filled our bowls and listened to him talk about plans for a dinner date and planning a trip out of the country.

* * *

I sat, remembering the last conversation with the man I married, that night we laughed, watched a movie, and cuddled for the rest of the night.

Days passed, and I hadn't slept good at all since the last conversation I had with Bosco. I wanted to scream, call my parents, and hide out until life went back to normal. Bosco ranted that night about how I had to work off a debt by getting back in good with my father-in-law. Based on my past relationship with the Fords, I expected to get pushback as soon as I tried to reach out. I smiled at Prince as he finished off his meal and curled close to me. If nothing else in this world, I knew Prince would be that one bright spot. I bent down and rubbed under his cheek like he likes, then the light went off on the coffee machine. After washing my hands I lifted the pot, filled up my thermos, and took some cinnamon and caramel creamer to top it off the way I liked. Today's schedule was full of interviews with major designers that were showcasing their designs at the fashion show. I blew on the steam to cool it down before sipping. I stretched my arms through my coat sleeves, sauntered back to the living room, grabbed my purse, keys, and work bag, then locked up behind me. I could barely move down the hall without encountering a guard doing a search of each room when they changed shifts. The one he called Keith only nodded; he probably felt the cold shoulder I gave him. He was the one who covered my mouth and knocked me out.

I strode toward my car, and his guard moved his hand in front of me to block my path.

"Ma'am you no longer are allowed to drive." He was casually amused.

I took an abrupt step back, wrinkling my nose. "Says who?" Disbelief was displayed on my face.

"Boss wants you to be driven around for your own protection."

"Protection...I don't understand," I stammered, expecting people not paying any attention. "I can drive myself."

Keith motioned toward a black-tinted town car across

the street. "Sorry, we have orders. For now, you are under strict rules."

The expression I wanted to give him would only hold me up further in a long argument, so I had to wait until another time to go back and forth. I sighed, marched through the parked cars, and went to reach for the handle when he stood in front of me.

"What now!" I barked, tossing my hands in the air. Every minute he irritated me only slowed me up.

"Women do not open doors, ma'am."

"A thug with manners, great..." I quipped.

He smirked, adjusted to the right, and let me climb in. I slammed it closed, and threw my arms over my chest in a pout.

Ring

Car tires screeched away from the curb as we left the block. I bit the inside of my cheek, impatient at the long, drawn-out ride to my office.

"Hello."

"Hey, I wanted to remind you that we have the interview scheduled in thirty minutes at the facility," Andrea, my editor, said quickly.

"Yes, I am on my way to them now, and then back to the office."

"Great, if we can have the interview to run before the fashion show premier, we will be on track to do on air questions and hopefully you will be ready for the camera."

"Uhmmm..."

"Come on Giselle, you are the best at the job," Andrea begged.

"Can I have some time to think it over? I'm really backed up with a few projects."

"Sure thing, just let me know by tomorrow." She hurriedly hung up.

"Tomorrow?" I groaned and sat back as we pulled up to the main hall of Chapel Rose Fashion House.

Keith came around to help me out. I ignored his hand, moved around him, strolled to the security booth, signed myself in, and grabbed a name badge.

"Giselle, welcome to Chapel Rose," the assistant greeted me, and I stretched my hand out toward her.

"Thank you for agreeing to the interview."

Kathy gestured to follow her. "I am big fan of your work, and when I saw the last story you did, I asked Rose if she'd be interested."

"Usually we get turned away." I chuckled, then sipped on my coffee.

"Kathy, will you make sure lunch is ordered for us, please?" Rose Thorn, owner and designer of Chapel Rose, stood from her chair at her design table and met us halfway. "Do you have any allergies, Giselle?"

I hoisted my bag on my shoulder. "None, thank you for asking."

"Giselle, nice to meet you, I'm Rose Thorn."

A smattering of pictures sat on each wall, showcasing her work over the years. Her staff seemed lovely and moved easily as she took time to talk with me.

"Pleased to meet you, Miss Thorn."

"Please call me Rose." Rose linked her arm in mine and walked us into her office.

The entire space was laid out like a true designer's dream, with a full runway in the middle of the room in shades of white and red. Her brand was known for incorporating leopards in some capacity. I was surprised the place wasn't filled to the walls. Lights beamed from the ceiling. A few people held up dresses, as her assistant talked on the phone and managed to keep things organized.

"Come have a seat. The food will be here shortly."

I laid everything down on the couch, then shuffled through my bag to pick up the recorder and notepad. Rose sat in the chair and crossed her legs, cupping her hands together.

"Chapel Rose is the number one brand everyone is looking forward to seeing, thank you again for this inter-view." I sat forward with a smile.

A knock came, and her assistant ambled inside, holding a few papers in her hand. "I need a signature, and I put in the order for your food."

"Thank you, Kathy," Rose replied, handing the files back to her.

"So, tell us about Rose Thorn."

Rose sighed, then grinned. "That's a loaded question, how long you got?" She laughed, drinking more of her coffee.

"I have time."

"Let me see, I guess you can say Chapel Rose started because I never saw myself in some of the clothes out here," Rose explained.

"Fashion Week is starting, and you are one of the top brands recognized by *Variety*, *Elle*, and *British Vogue*."

"*Blue Magazine* is one of my favorites." She beamed, excited to talk about our small-print magazine. It started out small and grew to be respected in the industry, and I was proud to be a part of what we brought to the table. Her announcement about our magazine being one of her favorites made me giggle.

"We appreciate having you as a reader."

"You actually started the press for my designs, truly grateful for the work you've done."

I held a hand to my chest in shock. "Really?"

Rose bobbed her head. "Yes, and that's why I requested you to come here and look at some of the pieces I have planned for the show."

"We kind of started out at the same time, so I saw you climbing the ladder like me," I confessed. Her announcement sent a warm feeling to my heart.

Today was a perfect opportunity to use the interview to escape without Keith noticing. For the longest time, I wanted to make time with Rose Thorn, but I had to make a quick exit to save myself from Bosco and his family.

"Uhh, Rose, do you have a restroom I could use?"

Rose leaned forward to pick up her food and took a bite. "Sure, it's down the hall on the left."

"Too much coffee running through me."

She tittered, rose from her chair, and went to one of her workers, who was holding up a few dresses.

I waited for a brief second to make sure Rose was occupied, slowly walked back in her office and swiped up my purse and bag, eased around the mannequin, and waved to Kathy her assistant.

Kathy shot a panicked look in my direction. "Hey, are you all right?"

"Yes, I need a huge favor." Heart lodged in my ribs, I clutched her left hand.

"Anything."

"A car is parked out front. It's my ex."

Kathy waved off the rest of my comment. "Say no more."

Relief trickled through my veins, even though I had to create a story.

"Can I go out the back and I will send Rose the inter-view questions later to answer?"

Kathy glanced over my shoulder at security. "No prob-lem. Should I call the police?"

"That would be amazing." I rushed to the employees-only area in the back, jogged to the exit, sprinted down the alley, peeked around the wall, and released a sigh. I continued to the next building and got to the corner, holding up my finger to hail the cab driving down the street.

"Where to, ma'am?"

"To Gold Coast Catering on 10th and Brand."

Ring! Ring!

An unknown number that I could bet belonged to Keith or his boss appeared on my phone. My cab driver arrived not long after. I handed over my last bit of cash, jumped out, and swiftly rushed inside, searching to see if I could spot Mallory.

One of her coworkers stood at the front putting up a display.

"Have you seen Mallory?"

She pointed to the back. "In the freezer."

"Thanks."

I followed another cook and saw Mallory come out of the freezer with a bag in her hand.

Mallory leaned forward to kiss me on the cheek. "Gigi, what are you doing?" She dropped it on the counter. "Shouldn't you be at work? I mean I usually have to pry you from the computer." She giggled.

"I ran away," I whispered.

Mallory looked left, then behind her and grasped my shoulder, pulled me to the corner near the fridge. "Ran away? From work?" She scrunched up her noise.

"The guy had a bodyguard drive me to work today, not

only that he expects me to get a million dollars to pay him back."

My sister laced our fingers and dragged me farther to the back corner of the kitchen. "Slow, down, take a breath."

"Mallory, you have to help me," I pleaded as I peered at the staff moving about like nothing was really going on.

"Gigi, please, you need to calm down."

I snatched my hands away. "You think I'm crazy!"

"First tell me about you running away."

While we were growing up, I always expected her to believe me, but she often needed long, drawn-out explanations that I had no time to give. I could see her wheels turning, and she was probably trying to plan what she would tell our parents.

"Hey, you can't go back there!" someone screamed. The doors busted open, causing everyone to jump back, scared.

My mouth dropped agape in shock. *How did he know I was here?* I thought.

Bosco stood with a deep crease in his forehead and narrowed eyes. Keith trailed behind him.

"Who the hell are you?" Mallory argued.

Bosco raised a finger to his lips, those perfect full lips that haunted my dreams formed into a thin line.

I jumped in front of her to block his view. "Mallory, please."

Bosco clenched his fists, stalked forward, and stared from Mallory to me.

"She doesn't know anything," I begged, shoved my sister farther back, and pleaded with my eyes for her to shut up.

A desperate look glazed over her face. "Gigi."

"Mallory." I grunted and clasped her hand from behind my back.

"Quiet," Bosco demanded, shoving his hands in his pockets.

I felt my throat tightened up.

"I will call the police." Mallory reached in her pocket and pulled out her cell.

Bosco reached around me to snatch it out of her hands, threw it on the ground, and stomped his foot on top.

"Oh, my God!" Mallory screamed as she bent down to grab what was left.

I yanked her back to stay behind me. "Bosco look." I held a hand up in the air.

He cocked his head to the side. "Shush, you had a chance, and you decided to disobey me."

I closed my mouth.

"Keith called me because he went to check on you, and you were nowhere in sight for the interview. So, the notion of you continuing to work seems unnecessary."

"That's my job!" I hissed.

"A job you claimed was important, but you ran off."

"Because—" Right as I got courage to answer him back, he interrupted.

"It's time to start."

"Start?"

My sister linked her arms on both of my arms. "Gigi, we can call the police or Daddy," she threatened.

Bosco chuckled at her comment. "Let me do the honors." The ego of this man was appalling.

Mallory and I watched as he grabbed his phone and dialed someone.

"We never call on the phone," a familiar voice spoke.

"Daddy?" Mallory and I said at the same time, peering at each other in shock.

Bosco smirked, hung up without an answer, and stuck

the phone back in his pocket, gesturing for everyone to step outside.

"I am not leaving my sister. Wait, you look familiar!" Mallory exclaimed.

I whirled around and faced her, then hugged her tight. "Mallory, it's fine. I promise."

Bosco narrowed his brows at me. "Keith, hold Mallory in the other room," Bosco commanded.

Mallory fought with Keith as he dragged her away. Bosco leered around the kitchen, then he picked the knife from the counter and twisted it left to right.

Bosco tapped the tip of the knife to check how sharp it was. "Gigi."

"Don't call me... Look Bosco I won't be able to get you the money."

He held the knife in between us. "I see."

I took a step back, and he moved forward. "Whatever you had with my husband is between you and the Ford family." It was like a weird dance that my mind couldn't stray from—even if it wanted to.

Bosco elevated the knife above my head and stabbed it in the wall. "I agree."

"So, you will let me go?" I gulped out the words, feeling tension in my heart as I tried to anticipate his next move.

"No." He smirked, removed the knife from the wall, and aimed it back at me.

I gasped, as the knife was a few inches from my neck. "Please, you have to understand."

Bosco snatched my hand and stared at my old wedding ring, then yanked it off my hand. "Again, you are telling me what I need to understand." Sneakiness crept across his face.

In the fashion world, you had to have a sense of boldness, and an attitude that no one could get one over on you —especially in a business that chewed up fresh talent. Every time somebody tried to test me and push my buttons, I held my own.

In that moment, my stance was stiff. I was unable to put up a big fight, but I willed myself. I extended my hand to grab my ring from him. "That's mine."

"He's been dead for four years and you still wear his ring." Bosco presented a defiant snarl.

"On special occasions."

Most of the staff were missing, and that left just us in the kitchen.

"I can probably get fifty grand for it," he nonchalantly said.

"That ring is worth three hundred thousand."

"Like I said probably fifty grand." He chuckled, took the ring, and dropped it in the garbage disposal.

"My ring!" I screeched, lunging to remove it out of the sink.

Bosco yanked me to his chest. "Let's go, it's trash now."

I balled up my fists and tried clawing out of his tight grip. "I hate you! That was the only thing left of Jason's," I sobbed, wiping away my tears with my palms. I felt hiccups starting up. I glanced over my shoulder one more time.

Keith came back to the kitchen entrance. Bosco nudged me to leave. Sweat seeped into my palms; anxiety built up in my nerves, and my stomach dropped at what was going to happen to me. *Will he kill me like they did Jason?*

An umbrella appeared to the right of me, held up to cover me. I gazed into the distance at the people moving along as normal.

Rain started to pour down heavier as we rode in the limo. My gut told me that I should have run out of state to keep my family safe. Complete silence filled the car ride, and the phone blew up, but I was too scared to answer. Mallory probably thought something happened and contacted my father.

"Where are you taking me?" I asked as I scrolled the text thread.

Mallory: *Call me.*

Me: *Take care of Prince for me.*

Mallory: *I will.*

He turned to look at me, eyes cased from the top of my head, down my body, and reached to grab my phone.

"That's my phone!"

"You will get it back."

"Are you going to kill me?"

Ignoring my question, he faced the front and talked to Keith.

* * *

Our short ride ended at a bridge. I gripped the door handle and peered out the window at the other cars moving past us like a limo on the side of a bridge was normal. Bosco hopped out of the car and went to rip open my door.

"No! Please, you don't have to do this."

Bosco knocked on the window. "Open the door or else your sister will get another visit from me."

I unlocked the door slowly. He shoved his hand forward, gripped me by the nape of my neck, and dragged me out of the car.

The waves rippled below.

"No! Bosco, listen."

"You had your chance."

I extended my hand and tried to shove him back. I stumbled to the side of the bridge. Perspiration prickled my body, and my heart plummeted into the pit of my stomach with the realization that no one could help.

"Second chances are for fools," he taunted.

From the corner of my eye, I could see a few people slowing down. "*Help!* He's trying to *kill* me!" I screamed, throwing my hands in the air to draw attention. My body felt heavier from him being pressed against my chest, and my screams turned into a moan as he kissed me.

His lips felt softer than Jason's.

Bosco crashed his lips on top of mine again, bringing on a weird, confused feeling that encompassed me. I was unable to control myself. On its own, my tongue submitted, along with my hands, which curled around his waist. I was momentarily out of my mind.

My eyes popped open. I tried to push him back. Bosco removed his hand from my neck, leaned beside my ear, and planted both hands on each side of me to block me from moving.

After he winked, he hitched my phone up in the air. "Those lips will get you in trouble."

Bosco tossed the phone in the water without any thought or guilt.

I swiveled around, my eyes panning from the water to him.

"Let's go."

"My phone!"

"It will be replaced."

"I had all my business contacts on there. My entire life was just thrown away."

Bosco ignored my comment and grasped my hand to walk back to the limo.

I laid a hand on top of the car and stopped. "Where are you taking me?"

"Home, you will have a new phone."

"Prince is probably not fed. I need to check on him," I lied, I already knew Mallory would be there for him.

His brows knitted together in question. "Prince?"

"My baby."

"The *fuck!*"

Chapter Six

Bosco

Keith tucked Giselle in the spare hotel suite with her baby—who I found out was a damn dog once she explained it. I'd never heard of them having a child, and thinking about someone like her letting Jason's bitch ass between her thighs pissed me off even more. My nerves were shot from hearing how she escaped and went to visit her sister; I wanted to kill her and fuck her at the same time.

My brother and Savio agreed that she was becoming a bigger problem for the family, and our time was too focused on her. Ultimately, she would be useful for me to get news on Steele and her father-in-law.

I was sitting next to my brother, Armani. I'd invited our cousins Savio and Sante, who had come to town with their wives. Giosuè was out to dinner with his wife. Some of the guys tagged along to a strip club, while waiting on Allen to get there.

We also got word that Steele was planning on hitting a few places with his gang, so I amped up security in case they made an appearance. Drinks were poured, and asses shook around the room. I kept my eyes straight as Allen approached security, and they patted him down, then allowed him past with his team.

"Bosco! If I didn't know any better, then I'd call you The Butcher." Allen chuckled.

It was the night after I had to put a scare in Giselle at the bridge, and I was not in the mood for Allen's jokes. The slight curve of Armani's top lip showed that he was just as annoyed as I was in Allen's company. Drinks flowed, and people got too comfortable for my liking; tonight, I was there to just close the deal and handle Giselle.

"Drinks on you, right?" Allen smirked, passing the bottle of vodka to his right-hand man.

"First drink on me."

Allen's head fell back in a loud laugh.

"How about we make it official? You remember my cousins from Chicago, Savio and Sante," I introduced them, refilling my glass.

"The Don and the underboss of the Calabresi family. I've heard good things about the Chicago family," Allen expressed.

"You can save the kissing up, Bosco agreed to increase product," Armani chided in his usual passive aggressive speech.

Allen raised a brow at the hint of disrespect in his direction.

Fighting with the Grazianos couldn't happen tonight; one enemy was enough. I stretched my hand out to stop Armani as he reached for his gun. Our eyes connected, and he nodded in understanding.

"Celebrate the increase Allen...my brother likes to get down to business." I sighed.

Allen gulped his drink down and winked at one of the

girls to get her to come over to him. He placed a few hundred dollars in her thong.

"While we visit and my little cousin is handling business, I have to let you and your boys know my reach extends beyond Chicago. I know Armani and Bosco hate for me to take over the conversation, but their brother is not here as the Don," Savio informed.

Sante, Savio, and Armani stared at Allen, waiting for a response. Allen's eyes lingered on the dancer coming to the stage. Stasia's music slowed down for her entrance, and the DJ gave her introduction and told everyone to have all their money ready.

Allen patted his lap for one of the dancers to come closer. "No disrespect, Bosco. Come on, we are friends."

I slouched forward with my hands on my knees and stared at him. "Tomorrow your men will have what they've asked for. Come up with any problems and you will find out my friendship has conditions."

Armani tilted his head at one of the groupies, and Allen stuck his hand out. I paused for a second, then shook hands.

"Ladies, show our guests why we're the best in town," I boasted, wrapped a hand around the back of Illana's head, squeezed her neck, and poured champagne down her throat.

Savio motioned for one of the girls to move around before she came closer. I admired him and my brother for being devoted to their wives. Marriage never looked fun, or like something that would work for me. The amount of travel and time that it took to make another person happy felt like it would be draining.

The shared kiss with Giselle today came out of nowhere, it wasn't planned. Her screams, and fighting me back, I had to try and distract people that started to slow down and wanted to help her.

Tired of being in Allen's presence and ready to check on my business, I got up and eased out of the party section. One girl stroked a hand down my chest and dick, then licked her lips.

"Not tonight, sexy."

She pouted and went back to her friend. I maneuvered down the hall to the steps, already knowing that Armani would be right on my heels. He and Sante followed me to my office and closed the door. I stood in front of the security cameras, monitoring the crowd and staff.

"First drop is in the morning around nine," Sante explained.

I marched to the bathroom in my office, turned on the light, and released my dick to take a leak. "Armani and I will be there to make sure it flows," I yelled through the door.

"Savio and I will join you," Sante agreed.

Right after I cleaned off my dick, flushed, and washed my hands, I stepped back over to my desk. "Did Giosuè tell you about Steele Graziano?"

"That's why I came here. I know you have the skills to run New York, just here to help." Sante snatched the cigar from Armani's hand.

Armani texted on his phone.

Sante focused on the screen, and Armani slouched down in the chair ready to go murder Allen even if he ever screwed us.

Sante clapped my brother on the shoulder.

"I have Giselle as the point person to get close to her ex-father-in-law."

"Giselle is the widow, correct?" Sante investigated.

I hated it whenever anyone brought up that she was Jason's widow; it made no sense why she would date—let alone marry—an idiot like him. I still had our kiss on my mind, and it really pissed me off how someone who I had barely seen in the last four years had such a hold in my brain. Remembering when I sprang up at her place, and her little fists drew up like angry stones, I chuckled to myself.

"Something funny?" Armani probed.

"No—and yes, she's his widow."

Armani handed his phone to Sante. "Giselle Ford, she's going to be our way. Plus, the underground fight clubs that Steele owns will get us closer to taking them down."

"Can she be trusted? Most of our women may come across weak, but they have fire in their bellies." Sante put out the flame on his cigar with both fingers and passed the cell back.

"Giselle can be controlled, I can guarantee it."

We had gotten information that Steele and his boys hung out at fight clubs, and we planned to check a few out. Using that form of entertainment to make money was at least exciting, but Jason and his father had lost a lot of money to them.

Armani pinched the bridge of his nose, staring at his cell. My little brother's temper was as bad as mine.

I stood and tapped the side of the chair to get his attention. "Who pissed you off?"

Armani turned his phone around to show a clip of Allen and Steele talking together in a heated conversation.

"When was it taken and where, because Mikell put people on Allen."

"Tech team said the bastards were together two days ago near our trucking business." Armani grimaced.

"He's trying to play you." Sante's jaw flexed, a tell that blood would be shed soon.

I took off my coat, then slid on my leather jacket and helmet. "Come on, I have my bike out back."

Armani held his phone to his ear. We jogged downstairs to the back exit. Mikell pulled up in the limo for Armani and Sante to jump in.

"Send a text to your brother."

Sante slid into the back seat. "Already sent. He's taking care of Allen's security team."

Mikell waited for me to hop on my bike.

I signaled a hand in the air to trail behind me. The streets were quiet, and I sped down the road and hit the gas with thoughts of how Allen and Steele got close to my place of business.

A red light slowed me down, and I felt my phone vibrate in my pocket. I took it out and saw a picture of Giselle at the hotel.

Me: Where the fuck did you get the photo?

Unknown: She's beautiful.

Someone had to be close enough to get a picture of her, which meant they followed us from her place to the hotel.

Me: Grazianos aren't stupid.

Unknown: Might want to tell your friend to be careful when she orders room service.

"Shit," I hissed, ignoring the light as it turned green and making a U-turn in the middle of the street. It made Mikell force a pileup as cars honked at him. A twenty-minute ride turned into ten, and I arrived at her floor with Mikell, Sante, and Armani behind me. I could admit that I had an aggressive temperament when I felt threatened, or someone I valued was threatened, but I knew neutral bargaining would have to be negotiated. With my lips pressed together in concentration, I removed the safety, tightened my grip, and leaned my ear to the door to check for any sounds.

"On three," I whispered, facing them with a hand in the air to countdown.

They nodded as I counted down, raised my leg, and kicked the door off the hinges.

"Arghh!" Giselle screamed and fell to the floor.

Mikell and Armani moved to the left, toward the bedroom.

I headed toward Giselle to help her stand. "Anyone here?" I inquired.

"No, what are you doing?" she fussed, smacking my hand away.

"Did you have anybody come up here?"

Her feminine scent engulfed me, her clean face free of makeup looked innocent and that was the most dangerous thing if I didn't handle her quickly.

"Room service. I mean Keith checked the guy out."

Armani and Mikell came in from the backroom. "Clear," Armani said.

Giselle crossed her arms and cocked her head to the side. "Who did you expect to be in there?"

I held my phone up to her face. "I received a picture of you tonight, seems like you've been found out."

Giselle tried to grab my phone, and I pushed it back into my pocket. "Get dressed. You're leaving."

With her hand planted on her hip, she frowned at me. "Where are you taking me?"

"My house."

I couldn't directly call her an enemy, but I was too cautious to be friends.

Silence filled the entire room.

"Bosco," Armani called my name.

I walked over to him. "Before you ask, I know what I'm doing."

"She could be setting you up." Armani stood there with a militant posture.

I gazed over his shoulder at Giselle as she paced back and forth, mumbling to herself.

"Best way to keep her safe until we get the rest of the money and find out what Steele is doing."

"Giosuè should know."

I sucked my teeth. "Giosuè will find out when I'm ready for him to be included."

"Hi, I'm Sante," Sante introduced himself, eyebrows raised in obvious pleasure.

I shook my head at my cousin as he talked with Giselle. "She won't be around long enough for you to be friends." The thought made my throat ache with regret when I saw her face drop at my statement.

"Rena and Mckayla might be helpful," Sante suggested.

I narrowed my eyes at him, dragging my tongue over my teeth.

"Who are they?" Giselle wondered.

I moved around Armani and nudged Giselle to the bedroom. "Go get dressed, pack your things. We leave in five minutes."

"What about Prince?"

"Who is Prince?" Armani asked.

"My baby." Giselle smiled.

I sighed in frustration. "Nothing."

The comment flew out of my mouth, and right then, an ugly little mutt pranced out of the bedroom and cuddled up at her feet.

Armani and Sante stared at me, then burst into laughter.

Giselle bent down and rubbed behind his ear, then walked back to the bedroom and managed to extend five minutes into thirty thanks to the questions she kept throwing at Keith and Mikell. As soon as I arrived home, Giosuè was on our line, yelling about the shit hitting the fan. Armani was able to calm him down, while I got her situated at the compound instead of my condo.

* * *

Loud shouts and cheers erupted around us as we walked around the fight club. Steele and his men were in the back corner with one of his fighters. I observed and waited until the ref made the call as one guy took too many punches to his chest.

"Fight, fight!" the crowd yelled.

"He's spotted us." Armani tapped me on the arm, then gestured to Steele as he tipped his beer bottle before taking a sip.

"Good."

Pop! Pop!

Everyone screamed and ran, shoving each other to get away from the gunshots.

I pulled Armani beside me, hand on his shoulder. "Keep cover, that motherfucker did this on purpose."

While one of the guys punched Mikell in the side of the head, Keith wrapped his hand around his neck and yanked him away. Sante and Mikell followed us down the hall as we chased Steele.

"Gun!" Sante shouted.

I ducked before the shot rang out.

Steele and his gang rushed out the exit and shot at him, missing him by an inch.

I moved slowly and waved for the crew to keep going. "Fuck!"

Armani texted rapidly on his phone, Keith and Mikell ducked outside to search.

"Get the tech team back on him," I demanded.

"Allen set us up." Sante sighed.

"He knew we'd want to run after that photo came in tonight." I considered what all this meant, more killing would leave us less focused on making money.

"Go home and rest, we have to regroup," Sante proposed.

Armani closed his phone. "Giosuè said he ordered a sit-down with Graziano."

I brushed my hand down my head. "Ford. We need to talk to Ford."

Sante extended his hand toward the fight club. "What do you want to do about this place?" Sante moved quickly.

"Burn it down."

"Witnesses?" Armani asked.

"Give them five minutes. If any of them refuse to leave, then make it look at like an accident," I suggested, stalking to my bike.

Keith and Mikell stayed behind with Armani. Sante jumped in the Range Rover that Keith had Giselle stashed in and came up beside us on the main road in the direction of our home. Sante and Savio were staying at home with Giosuè and their wives.

We made it to the gate at my home. It spread wide as I drove up to the arched waterfall and parked. The security lights turned on as I turned the engine off and sprinted upstairs. I slid my key in and unlocked the door to a quiet hallway and living room. I turned to head into the kitchen to find no one.

Talk came from the movie room. I charged in to see Giselle with my housekeeper Yun holding a tray of food, and that damn dog on top of my couch like a damn baby.

I inhaled a shuddering breath to control my temper. "Yun, can you give us a second?"

"Yes, Mr. Calabresi." Yun smiled and strode away.

Giselle turned her back to me and I shut the door after Yun left, flipping the lock.

"We need to talk."

"I know what you want me to do and I agreed already." Giselle never faced me.

I snapped my fingers in her face. "Tomorrow you will have to talk with the Ford family."

"Okay."

My brow hiked at her agreement. "This is very serious, I hope you know that either you help get my money back or die."

Giselle wiped a tear that fell down her cheek. "Fine."

"It's important that Ford believes everything you tell him, first thing is that you knew they were taking money from our family."

Her head whipped around fast in a glare. "You want me to lie and blackmail him?"

"I do."

She got up, and the damn dog growled at me. "He's going to know I'm lying and kill me."

I twisted around to leave and reached for the knob. "Lying seems like one of your best traits."

"I want to speak to my family."

"Call."

"Not the same."

"Get through tomorrow and I will take you to see them."

"Is my dad really on your payroll?" Giselle probed, bending down to pick up her dog. "Tell me the truth."

I stalked out and called over my shoulder, "See you in the morning and keep that dog outside."

"What?!" Giselle barked, running up and pulling me by the shoulder to face her.

I glanced down at her hand, then back to her face, and she removed her hand.

"He's not an outside dog."

"Not my problem."

"Prince is my baby; you can't put him out."

I stepped around her. "Watch me."

Yun swiped the counter with the rag, tossed the remnants in the trash can, and smiled at me. "She's a nice girl, Mr. Bosco."

"Told you to call me Bosco."

"Your dinner is in the microwave. I will be back in a week. Are you really going to put her dog outside?"

"Please, Yun—not you, too."

Yun had worked with me for years and knew animals had no place in my home.

"He's sweet, maybe think it over before you decide." Yun giggled.

"Thanks Yun, already full and this is not doggy daycare."

I walked backwards out of the kitchen, stepped on the elevator in the corner, and headed up to the third level of my home.

Once I shrugged off my leather jacket, holster, and gun, I kicked off my shoes and turned on my phone to stare at the security cameras. She was still holding the damn dog in her hands and talking to Yun animatedly. I closed the video, lifted my shirt, threw it in the hamper against the wall, unzipped my jeans, and trudged to the bathroom. I turned the shower to the highest level, and steam filled the room. I leaned my head against the wall as the water poured down my back, and I closed my eyes.

Tomorrow's a big day. A clear head is how I should deal with Steele Graziano and his people.

Chapter Seven

Giselle

My large shades covered my eyes. I put my hair in a high bun and continued to listen to my sister bitch and moan about what happened at her job. Mallory decided to call me at seven in the morning and force me to hear how her boss wanted to fire her because of the issues I brought to their business. They reminded her of how I was on TV as the witness at the bakery shooting, and our parents wanted to know why I missed their family dinner. Today was the day they were leaving for their anniversary trip, and I wanted to see them before the flight.

I stepped out of the bedroom and waited for Mallory to finish, so I could open my mouth to speak—until I became speechless at a half-naked Bosco, standing with a cup of coffee in his hands and staring at the TV screen on the wall. I ambled toward him and saw what was on screen; it was the bedroom I slept in, and other parts of the house. Prince followed me, and I smiled. Whatever Bosco said about him went in one ear and out the other because Prince went wherever I went.

"You spied on me," I argued. I felt my privacy was disturbed.

"I hope they brought breakfast," he said, inclining his head toward two beautiful women, followed by Keith, Mikell, and the other gentlemen from yesterday, marching in his house.

Bosco leaned over the banister and everyone froze.

"Hey Bosco, and to your friend," the blonde woman spoke.

"McKayla, Rena good morning." Bosco cheesed like a teenager, and I wanted to smack it off his face.

"Who's your friend, Bosco? I hope you covered her cab ride this time," the redhead rambled.

"I'm not a hooker!" I shouted, offended at her statement.

"*Grhhh...*" Prince barked, and I leaned down to pick him up, forgetting about my sister.

"Rena be nice," the one that introduced himself as Sante said to her.

Bosco swirled around and headed back to his room.

"Gigi! Hello," Mallory yelled through the phone.

"Mallory, I have to call you back." I walked to the elevator, irritated that he looked good and was allowing these women to believe I was a hooker.

As soon as I stepped out of the elevator, I ambled toward the kitchen, ignoring all the stares and picking up a thermos to make tea.

"Hi, I apologize for my friend. My name is Mckayla. I'm married to Savio." She nudged her friend to speak up. "This is my best friend, Rena, and she's married to Sante."

Mckayla stretched her hand toward me, and I accepted with a curved top lip. If I could be nice to the women, then maybe I could get a friend on my side.

"Giselle. Nice to meet you both," I replied, set the pot on top, and flipped the burner on high.

Rena stood at the side of the island. Mckayla sat down in the chair. Sante shook his head at his wife, and the other guys walked away.

"Giselle, you seem familiar," Mckayla said.

I shrugged my shoulders, put Prince on the ground, and pulled him near the water bowl that Yun had set out for him. "I might have a familiar face."

"No, she's right; I've seen you before. Are you a model?" Rena asked, rubbing Prince's head.

After pouring hot water in my thermos, I added the tea bag and let it cool off, blowing on the top. "I write for *Blue Magazine*'s fashion section."

Mckayla gasped and snapped her fingers. "Oh right, I love that magazine, huge fan."

"Thank you." I smiled, watching Prince eat.

"You two have a lot in common Mckayla," Rena blurted.

Mckayla stood with her hands on top of the counter. "Rena." Mckayla sighed, gazing down at Prince. "He's cute."

"Thank you."

"Mckayla is a reporter—well, she was, until she got married and became a stay-at-home mom," Rena explained, giving up all Mckayla's personal business.

I poured more honey in my tea. "Really, a reporter?"

"Nothing like fashion; we mostly did news." A faint flush tinged her cheeks.

"That's amazing, I would love to read some of your work."

"Mckayla hates to gloat, but I will because she needs to remember how fabulous she really is and Savio should be grateful that she married him," Rena teased. Mckayla giggled at her friend as Savio and Bosco shuffled in the kitchen.

Savio moved behind Mckayla and kissed her on the cheek. "Shut up, Rena." Savio and Rena had brother-and-sister chemistry.

Rena flipped him off.

My eyes lingered on Bosco, dressed in a black T-shirt, jeans, and a leather jacket, with his helmet in his hand.

"Rena likes to talk trash, which means she likes you. Ignore her, and you will be fine," Bosco expressed.

Rena poked her lip up in a snarl.

"Bosco leave my wife alone." Sante wore a fawny beige wool coat. Each guy had a distinct style that matched their personality.

The front alarm let us know another guest stepped inside and my eyes beamed wide at the man that resembled Bosco when he entered the kitchen. From his dark hair, six feet in height, and broad shoulders.

Rena jumped off the chair and ran into his arms. "Giosuè, I haven't seen you in forever."

"Damn," I muttered, and all eyes stared back at me with a smirk.

Giosuè wrapped an arm around her shoulder and kissed her on the forehead. "Rena, you look beautiful, as always."

"Penelope let you out of the house?" Sante joked.

Giosuè glared at him and looked up at me. "Penelope understands when the family has a problem, we all work together."

"Giosuè, I want you to meet Giselle," Bosco introduced us.

I sank my teeth in my lower lip, feeling his cold eyes on me.

"The cars are ready." Armani popped in behind him.

Prince barked at them again. I bent down and picked him up.

Bosco aimed an arched brow in my direction, and I avoided his angry, heartless presence.

Rena stood on her toes and kissed Sante on the lips. "Well, we plan on going to get our hair and nails done while you men go to work."

I planted him behind the gate in the corner.

"Giselle is coming with us," Rena announced.

Mckayla held her hands up in prayer. "Bosco, let us enjoy her for a day and then you can deal with your business later."

Rena winked at me. "Yeah, it would be fun to meet the girl you have in your home."

"She's here for business, and nothing more," Bosco reminded me.

Rena shoved Bosco in the shoulder. "Calabresi men tend to downplay their feelings," Rena teased.

"She won't be around long enough to be friends with you," Bosco exposed, and my stomach dropped at his confession.

Mckayla gasped and Rena's eyes scanned from me to him.

I cleared my throat. "It's okay, I will be fine." My fate was already sealed when I married Jason and learned of his dealings.

Sante whispered in his ear, and he nodded.

"Go with them and security will be tight, don't try and run," Bosco spat.

Rena, Mckayla, and I walked out of the kitchen and to the front of the house, while the men deliberated. I jumped in the back of their car. Rena turned to face me as Mikell started the car to back out of the driveway.

"Giosuè seems to be upset with you," Mckayla said.

"My first time meeting him. I know his brother forced me to stay with him."

Rena removed her lipstick out of her purse and checked her makeup. "They're in a weird business that leaves them with trust issues, you will learn."

"I tried to run away."

Rena puckered her lips and put her things back, then cupped my hand. "You are the not the first."

During the car ride, we talked about my upcoming fashion article, and the fashion show that I planned to attend. Bosco was still not aware, and I planned to try to get him to agree if I could get him the money back sooner. Mikell stopped in front of the nail shop that Mckayla informed me she frequented when she came to town. She climbed out, and Rena and I followed, looking around the area.

"Have you ever been to Brooklyn?" Rena quizzed.

"A few times when I was younger."

"The best place to get your nails done is Sky High." Rena locked her arm in mine. Keith and Mikell followed behind and checked with the manager—I assumed to see if there were any back exits.

"I tried to run off on my husband plenty of times, Bosco will be fine." Their stories of the men in their lives really made me wish I had started off on a better foot with Bosco.

I giggled at her statement. "Thanks."

Rena linked her arm in mine. "So, what job do they want you to do?"

I remember doing simple things like self-care, and now it was indeed a luxury to get space alone.

The nail tech gestured to take a seat in the front section, I slipped my shoes off and got comfortable.

Keith and Mikell walked back outside and stood in front of the building.

"My husband stole money from them, and he wants me to get it back."

Rena and Mckayla glanced at each other.

"What?"

"Nothing, just be careful," Mckayla said. She checked us in with the nail tech and she pointed us to our section.

"Do you think he would kill me?" I whispered.

"Calabresi business can be complicated." Rena sat forward and put her feet in the water to prepare for her pedicure. The girls and I went back and forth for an hour on how they dealt with their husbands and living in the shadows of the Calabresi name. Funnily enough, I was glad that Bosco and I had no type of feelings for each other—I mean, the kiss he gave me was the best kiss I'd ever had in my thirty years, but I knew it was fake; even the way he lightly choked me, and the feeling of his body against mine, were just to distract any eyes that were on us. He would never be a man I could fall in love with and call my "forever."

"I need to use the restroom."

Rena slid up to stand. "Do you need us to come with you?"

"No, I will be fine." I liked how they hadn't judged me and were open to giving me a chance, as compared to the men in his family.

I washed my hands in the bathroom sink and stared in the mirror. The days had gotten longer as I tried to gain my freedom from him.

I turned and unlocked the door, then jumped back in shock.

"Corbin."

"Giselle, we can't talk here. I need you to come with me," my ex-father-in-law blurted out, looking behind himself. His hair was grayed a little more, but he was still tall, with a thin build and piercing blue eyes.

"How did you get in here?" I quizzed.

"Not the time. We have to leave, or they'll kill you."

"I have tried to call you for weeks," I fussed.

Corbin said, "I apologize, but it's not safe for us to talk here."

Corbin grabbed my hand and yanked me down the hall. I wasn't able to pick up my purse or signal I was in trouble as the loud music blasted in the air.

He shoved me inside the burgundy Ford truck, then slammed the door. "Go, we only have a few minutes before they notice her missing," Corbin demanded.

I scooted closer to the window and reached for the handle to try to escape. "Corbin, where is the money?"

His blinked rapidly. "Shut up!"

Corbin never liked me. Jason gave so many excuses, but my working-class family mixing with his wealthy one was the main problem in his father's opinion. I wasn't good enough for his son.

Corbin answered his ringing phone. "She's with me, we're about five minutes away. Have my money."

I held a hand to my chest. "Corbin..." My heart gave a lurch.

He leered at me.

"Jason stole money from the wrong people."

His driver cut across three lanes of traffic, almost careening over the median.

Corbin laughed and hung up the phone. "Jason only did what I said to do."

"A million dollars and he robbed trucks." My flesh crawled just being this close to him.

"We were broke and needed money."

My voice rang out like a pealing church bell announcement of the second coming. "Give him the money back."

"I don't have it anymore." He shrugged like it was a simple thing.

"What about my family?"

His grin washed away like chalk drawings in spring rain.

Suddenly a blast of bullets wheezed by from all sides of the car.

Ratttta! Rattta!

I slumped down in my seat to get low and stay safe as they weaved around to avoid gunshots. "Arghhhh!" I screamed at the window being shattered and wished I could stay back at the house with Prince.

Corbin looked through the window. The driver changed lanes, and the other guard rolled the window down and shot back. The window shattered behind me, and I scrambled to get down to the floor.

"Pull over!"

I heard someone shout.

Corbin's face turned red in anger. He motioned to his driver to move to the corner of the stop sign. I crawled up onto the seat and jumped back as the door was snatched open, and I saw a pair of familiar black gloves and a black helmet as Bosco appeared in front of me.

Bosco raised the gun in the air at my face.

"Where's my money, Corbin?"

Pop! Pop!

"Oh, my God!" I dropped down to the floor of the car,

and before Bosco could shoot at Corbin, more bullets whizzed our way.

"Come on. Get on my bike!" Bosco shouted.

"I've never ridden on a bike." I hesitated.

Bosco wrapped both hands around my waist, planted me on the back of the bike, and he got in front. I looked to the right and saw Rena and Mckayla in the car with Keith and Mikell, behind I saw some other men on bikes.

Corbin's car sped off.

Sirens blared in the air. Bosco hauled me away as some of his people lingered behind, still shooting. I clung to his waist, closed my eyes, and took deep breaths to control my anxiety as we sped through traffic, moving through the streets. My stomach was a ball of knots. I'd almost gotten kidnapped, and I was scared of who he was talking to on the phone. I felt silence around me and opened my eyes. The bike slowed down. I popped up and saw that we were moving through the woods.

"Where are you taking me?"

"Our cabin."

As soon as the bike stopped, I jumped off and tried to run, but this man blocked me from leaving.

"No." Tears pooled in my eyes.

Bosco clenched a hand around my wrist, picked me up, and slung me over his shoulder. I was grateful for the support. The girls jumped out of the car and charged at him. Their husbands tried to hold them back.

"Bosco leave her alone!" Rena yelled.

Bosco let me down and pointed to the chair. I scanned the area. There was nothing but an empty room with a table in the corner. The building had large windows and was at least two stories tall.

"Sit and tell me what Corbin said."

More footsteps echoed on the wooden floor.

"We could have talked back at your house."

"Fuck you! Motherfucker!" shouted a guy who Keith was dragging inside. Keith slammed him to the floor, and blood seeped down his face.

"Bring him over here," Bosco demanded.

Giosuè and Savio stood in the back, Mckayla and Rena tried to push forward, and Sante nudged them to stay still.

"Fuck! Steele's going to kill you bitches," the guy grunted, slouching in the chair and grinning.

Bosco bent down and faced him. "Where's your boss?"

He stayed quiet.

Bosco stood, reached behind his back, removed his gun, and shot him between the eyes.

"Oh, God!" I cried, jumping out of my seat. I had never seen anyone killed in front me before except for my husband.

Bosco marched over to me and leaned forward, holding the gun under my chin with a hard glare.

"No more running, Gigi."

My eyes widened as he called me by my nickname.

Sante let Rena and Mckayla go and they rushed to me and helped me stand up as Bosco stalked to the door and left.

"Shush...Bosco is the underboss, you have to understand," Rena informed.

* * *

A warm bath and a glass of wine helped release some of the stress from the shooting. Bosco and I hadn't spoken since the cabin, and I liked it that way. He felt like I was hiding something, and I felt like he was thinking of any excuse to kill me —whether Jason was to blame or not.

The bubbles in my bath faded away. Steam filled the room. I drank the rest of the red wine and leaned over the tub to put it on the floor. I stood and unplugged the tub, watching the water drain, then picked up my towel and dried off. I sauntered into the bedroom and jumped back in surprise; Bosco was sitting on the edge of my bed.

Bosco met my eyes moodily. "Get dressed. We have company."

I drew my face away from him and went to a bag of clothes on the chair to find something to wear. "Who?"

"Your father."

"My dad?" I rushed to the door and paused, looking down at the towel and backing away to close the door. Then I whipped around and stared at him. "What is my father doing here?"

Bosco looked down at my bag of things. "He wants to talk to you."

I made a face. "He's supposed to be out of town."

"It was postponed."

Both of us stared down at the towel I wore.

I cupped my forehead, mouth dry and hands sweaty. "I need to get dressed."

Bosco rose from the bed, walked up to me, and stared down from my feet up to my blushed face. "You have five minutes."

I clamored around the dresser and closet to find a pair of pants and a large shirt to throw on. I prayed that I could get him to let me leave with him.

Chapter Eight

Bosco

Hours Earlier, at the Trucking Company

Allen and his men parked and stepped out of their vehicles, carrying bags that held what should have been my money for the product that we increased. The truck backed up, and one of the soldiers unhooked the lock and shoved it open.

"I hope you enjoyed your night."

"It was special, the girls were perfection. Here's all the money for today."

I cocked my gun, and his men stared, blocking him from me.

"Steele."

"Who?" Allen grinned.

"Steele Graziano and Corbin Ford."

Allen snapped his fingers and stepped up to the gun. "Money is my motive, why do you care what Steele and Corbin are doing?"

Another truck arrived and started to unload regular stacks of canisters filled with clothes and appliances for different stores.

Allen raised both hands. "I'm not the enemy."

"And this photo?" I held up the screenshot of him and Steele.

His brows shot up. "He wanted to talk business."

"What business?" I seethed.

His crew zipped up the bags. "Something that will bring us all more money. Looks great. I have to leave."

"Allen, if I find out you're involved in trying to take us down with him, then I will kill you."

Allen's men started loading up the crates. I watched all twelve fill the trunks of their cars and slam them shut. I turned my back to head back in when I heard the cock of a gun and scrambled to get behind a barrel of crates.

"Steele's on his way to get our girl! Fuck you, Bosco," Allen shouted, blasting his assault rifle.

"Get down!" I yelled, shooting back and hitting one of his men before they could get in the car.

Armani ran toward me. "Bosco!"

Time felt like it stopped when I saw him take a shot in the arm and fall.

"Get my little brother."

Allen drove off, and I ran with the gun in the air, sending more bullets into the back of his car. I was even more agitated. "Giselle." I ran back to Armani and helped him stand up.

"Go, I'm good."

I reached in my pocket and checked my cell. I saw that her location was on the main road, not the nail salon.

"Steele is a dead man." I raised the phone to my ear and

dialed Keith's number. It rang for a few minutes, and he finally answered.

"Boss we're tracking them on the road," Keith blurted. There was loud yelling in the background.

"On my way, stay with them."

* * *

Present Time

Aaron pointed a finger in my face. "My daughter should not be involved in any of your shit."

When the shootout made it to the TV, I got a call from her father, who wanted to see her in person. I tried to avoid the meeting, but Giosuè said it was best to keep him on our side, so I agreed and drove there alone.

I counted in my head to keep my cool. "Be careful; we know you're not all clean."

"Dad," Giselle said.

Aaron turned and held his arms open for Giselle. "Baby, you okay?"

Giselle sobbed in his arms. "I wanted to keep you and Mom from this mess, I know I've let you down."

Her father kissed the top of her head. "Gigi, you could never let us down. Are you hurt?"

"No, I was—"

"Giselle." The less Aaron knew about today's activities the better.

Giselle wiped her tears and stood. "I'm fine, Dad. How is Mom?"

Once again, that stupid dog she loved appeared, and this time, he stood in front of me with his tongue out. I wanted to kick him away but thought better of it.

"She wants you to come and see her, plus your sister is

angry about someone taking you from her job." Aaron's eyes flicked over to me.

"Giselle owes us since her husband is not here to get it back."

"She doesn't have that type of money, and you know it," Aaron hissed, pushing her behind him, like I wouldn't be able to touch her.

I crossed my arms over my chest. "Gigi, come here."

Giselle froze at my words.

"Bosco she's my little girl and you can't have her." Aaron's words hummed in the air.

I crept across the short distance. "She is here to get my money from Corbin and then she can leave."

"For how long?" Aaron checked.

Prince followed me to the bar.

"Not sure. We had a few hiccups, and I need the police reports blocked."

"As a retired cop I can't just get access to this stuff."

I motioned to the door. "Find a way. Now that family visit is over, you can go."

Giselle gritted her teeth, cut her eyes in my direction, then moved to hug her father and kiss him on the cheek. Something about her hugging another man, even if it's her father, irritated me. When Corbin kidnapped her and forced her in his car a spark of rage filled my chest. I hated anyone touching something of mine.

You kissed her one time.

I watched them go back and forth for a few moments. He kissed her forehead and stepped back, dragging his gaze in my direction. "If anything happens to my daughter, Bosco," Aaron threatened—even though he had a vested interest in making money on the side.

I cocked my head to the side, sizing him up. "Does your daughter know you covered up Jason's murder?"

Gigi stumbled back, out of his hold, shaking her head in confusion. "You're lying. Tell him it's not true."

Aaron held his hands out to caress her cheek. "Giselle, back then..."

Giselle tossed her hands in the air. "Dad, tell me the truth."

He bit down on his lower lip and grunted. "Gigi, four years ago I confronted Jason on what he did and told him to put the money back, and not send information to their enemies."

"Jason was too stupid to listen to him, and we found out and killed him. Your father got the call from me, and he came to clean up the scene."

"Corbin...Corbin was talking on the phone with someone about bringing me to them," she mumbled.

"Using my daughter as bait won't get you money," Aaron spoke.

A sharp gasp left her.

"I suggest you continue to run interference so our business doesn't get on the radar of the local police."

Aaron mostly reported to Giosuè or Armani. Our interactions weren't the best, and we had clashed a few times because he took a few of my men to jail on petty crimes.

"Stop it! Both of you are using me, and I can take care of myself. Dad, go celebrate your anniversary; Mom is looking forward to the two of you being together. Corbin will still be here." Giselle marched toward the bar, lifted a bottle of whiskey, poured a shot, and downed it.

I could tell by the fire in her eyes at me saving her earlier—a flicker of need, her hold around my waist, other women never saw that side of me. Women got their nut then left me alone, only one or two got to swing back in my bed.

Aaron left swiftly. Giselle marched in front of me with her finger in my face, sneering.

"Dispel any other problems, I am here to get your money back, leave my family alone."

"I like the fire in you, make sure you tell Daddy you got a new Daddy now."

She raised a hand to slap me. "Fuck you Bosco."

I grasped her wrist. "I bet you're used to men giving in to your spoiled ass. Not me." I ran a hand down her cheek, moved to the side of her face, and whispered in her ear, "Tell me, Gigi—is that pretty pussy wet for me?" I smiled and licked my lips.

Even though she tried to hide a hint of arousal, I could smell it on her since we were so close. "Ugh, let me go."

Prince barked, acting like her bodyguard.

"What time is your work thing?" I dismissed him, then watched her bend down and play.

He was hoisted in her arms.

"Why?"

"Because Corbin finally agreed to my demands, I have to set up security around the area."

"None of your bullshit should be happening at my place of business."

The pulled shades blotted out the glow from the lamp that hit her skin. All's fair in money and war, Aaron should have reminded his family.

Maybe if I gave her a little wiggle room, she'd lean more in my favor. Time was running out, and I wanted Steele's head. Since Gigi had been with us, I had seen her take on a fighter stance; maybe she felt like she had to compete with me, but I was still in charge.

"Remember why you're here."

"Ooh, I have no doubt of what I am doing here." Gigi scoffed, jerked out of my grip, stomped away, and moments later a door slammed.

Yun peeked in the living room with my cell in her hand. "Mr. Giosuè is calling."

"Thank you."

"Should I plan for dinner to be just you."

"Cook enough for two, just put her plate up. You can take off for the night."

"Great see you tomorrow, sir."

I nodded, holding the phone to my ear. "Yeah, Giosuè."

* * *

Giosuè stood outside the warehouse and waited for me to arrive, along with Armani and Nero. Sante and Savio greeted us. I glanced around at the extra henchmen and smirked.

"I could have handled it alone."

"We are family. You're in charge; we're just here for backup," Savio informed me, trailing beside Giosuè and into the warehouse.

I loomed closer, fury in my belly at the two people hanging from the ceiling. The Graziano gang really thought that they could shoot at us in the bakery and live to talk. Both men were stripped down to their boxers and hanging from their arms, already bloodied and bruised.

"Who started without me?"

My whole family shrugged their shoulders in avoidance.

Giosuè pushed both hands in his pockets. "They tried to kill my baby brother. I had to get a few hits in first."

Armani moved closer and lifted the hatchet from the wall. He had been with me when everything went down with the robberies and the bakery shooting.

"Where's Steele and Titus?" Armani barked.

Both men squirmed with wide eyes. I gritted my teeth, still not giving up any information. Armani raised the hatchet and swung at the shorter soldier who had tried to take my head.

"Arghhh! P-P-Please," he begged, watching his leg fall to the ground. Blood squirted everywhere. Slowly, his eyes started to close.

"Keep him alive," I said.

My guys smacked him on the cheek and Armani chuckled at his friend trying to get out of the chains.

Rattaa! Ratta!

"Get down!" I shouted, lifted my gun, and started blasting at the front door.

"Mgrhhhh!" Graziano's man tried to yell for help.

I sent a bullet to his head and ran toward the side window. A few bullets sliced through the building, hitting both their men in the back of the head. Savio and Sante went to the back of the warehouse and crept outside. Giosuè patted me on the shoulder and motioned toward the right window at a man standing outside with an automatic weapon. I slipped around him, dropped to the ground, shot him in the foot, and watched him fall. Armani yanked the door open, blasting his shotgun. Giosuè jumped up and held him back.

"Graziano's coming for you!" One guy drove off in a white pickup truck.

"Nero get me the address on that car!" I shouted.

"Already locating now, waiting on DMV to confirm," Nero expressed.

The walls were covered in bullets, tables were turned over, doors barely stood in one piece, and most of the cars had bullet holes or flat tires.

"I want to hit him back where it hurts."

Savio lifted his brow. "He's got a few blocks we can't touch without starting a war."

"Graziano is all about money and appearances. He has some nightclubs, let's shut them down."

Armani nodded and shifted the wooden chair upright. "Tonight."

"Yeah, ride out and send a message."

"Be careful. We can't make a big scene." Concern grew on Giosuè's face.

"He owns a few check-cashing places. We can hit each one at the same time and make him regret coming at us."

"I got it!" Nero typed on his phone.

I felt my cell vibrate, and I slipped it from my jacket.

"I've seen him before." Savio leaned over Nero's shoulder.

"He was with Allen at the strip club," I snapped, aggravated that Allen thought he can play me.

Nero started the car. I ran to my bike and trailed behind, heading to the first address on the list of businesses. Armani drove the Range Rover that had gotten shot up, and Giosuè rode with Nero, while Savio and Sante rode in the car with their own team.

No sooner did we make it back to the city than we pulled up to the check-cashing place that Steele owned. All the lights were off, and the streets were empty. I hopped off, ran to the back, picked the lock, and stalked inside. I turned behind me at the flicker of a light in my face. Armani came in, followed by Nero. The place seemed like it was decorated back in the late '90s, with floral-patterned carpets, unfinished paint on the walls, and cabinets barely holding together, with one or two legs held up with books.

I motioned to the wall. "Hit the safes. If they have an alarm, then we only got a few minutes before the police arrive."

"Savio and Sante hit up the clubs." Nero turned his phone to show a video of people running out of the club screaming and crying.

"He's going to be on us soon."

"Better for us," I said, starting to kick over the chairs, then picking up the registers and tossing them to the ground. Armani held the hatchet in his hand and opened the safe. He was grabbing bags of money when we heard sirens nearby.

"Shit, we got to go," I whispered.

"What are we going to do with the money?" Nero inquired.

I smiled. "I have the perfect idea."

I grabbed two bags and ran out of the building as Nero shot out the front windows. I tossed the bags in the back of Armani's car and jumped on my bike, leaving the first location. At two in the morning, we finished stealing from five of his locations and piled the money together and laid it out on the tarmac.

"How much did we get from him?" Armani asked.

"A small amount compared to what his drug business runs. He mostly uses the place for laundering. It looks like about five million."

"Have one of them ride my bike back."

Armani drove us to the neighborhood where the shootout happened. It was going on eight in the morning, and a few places were already open. I removed the black mask and rode shotgun. He parked in the middle of the street. Nero whistled, and our soldiers came out from the cars and started to grab bags and drop stacks of money at each door. I smiled at the shocked faces of people crying, excited at the free money they'd received. Afterwards, we drove away and dumped the rest near his territory. I stepped out of the car, poured lighter fluid on top of the bag, and lit a match.

"What the fuck? Steele's going to kill you!"

"He knows where to find me, stop acting like a bitch and come forward," I taunted, flicked the lighter, and watched the money burn.

None of his men made a move, and I winked as Nero left and headed back to my house to let my team know that I would be out of commission. I brushed a hand over my bike, parked in front of my house, and walked up to unlock the alarm. Exhausted from the night before, I kicked off my shoes and jacket and fell in the middle of the bed.

"Bosco!"

"Mr. Calabresi."

Yun and Gigi knocked on my door. Not getting any sleep, I rolled over and watched the door open to see confusion on their faces.

"What?"

"The police are downstairs." Yun fidgeted with her hands nervously.

I slid up against the headboard and picked up my cell to check the cameras. "Police?"

"They want to talk to you." Giselle grinned, filed her nails, probably getting a kick out this moment.

I yanked the covers back, stood, stretched my arms, and slowly grabbed a shirt and jogging pants as she stared. I plucked her nose, and she came out of her daze. We went to see why the police had come to my home uninvited. Three men stood at the door, and one of them had a piece of paper in his hand.

"Can I have a reason why you're at my house?"

"We need to speak with you about an arson," the officer stated.

Chapter Nine

Giselle

"Arson," Rena repeated.

I was still in shock from Bosco being taken to jail on the charge of possible arson. I was at work—well, technically, at the fashion show. I hadn't talked to him in a few days since everything happened, and I was focusing on my career again. For the most part, I agreed to Keith and Mikell staying out front, but the girls would be sitting in the front row with me to watch the fashion show. There was so much press, and big-name celebrities were lining up. Rose offered me a private showing beforehand, and I let the girls look at all the pieces, so we weren't completely new to what she'd be modeling.

The lights turned down low, the music started, and people started to get prepared as the announcer came up to the mic.

I checked my phone, looking down to see a text from Corbin.

Corbin: *Giselle, I know it was bad, but I want to make amends.*

Me: *You tried to have me killed.*

Corbin: *I promise to explain everything.*

Rena laid a hand on my shoulder. "Everything okay?" When they received the invite, they were so excited and dressed to impress. Rena was in an opal drop-torso dress. Mckayla was in an olive suede jumpsuit.

I tucked a piece of hair behind my ear. "Sorry, yeah, a friend catching up."

Mckayla leaned forward. "That two-piece pant set would look good on you, Rena."

Corbin: *Where are you?*

I listened to the girls go back and forth.

Me: *At a fashion show.*

Corbin: *There's something of Jason's I want to show you.*

I bit my bottom lip and glanced up at the girls taking pictures.

Me: *Come to Fourth and Main near Wall Street.*

Corbin: *Great, see you soon.*

"Rose Thorn has the next evening gown portion for all sizes. Prepare yourselves," the announcer said.

Corbin: *I'm here in the back.*

I stood and Rena grabbed my wrist.

"Where are you going?"

"Bathroom, be right back." Bile threatened to spew from keeping the secret of Corbin coming there. So much adrenaline ran through me from my arguments with Bosco about him not coming home early, and the police showing up the next day. It would have been a great escape if I told the police, but the look in his eyes told me that I wouldn't last a minute under police custody.

"Hurry, the party is after this, and I am ready to drink." Rena grinned and high-fived Mckayla.

I moved through the crowd and waved at a few

coworkers and other established designers, until I made it to the green room for the models. Everyone ran around busily, trying to get dressed and get their makeup and hair done.

The buzz on my phone caught my attention.

Corbin: *Turn around.*

I swiveled around and saw Corbin wearing a black trench coat, shades, and a hat, standing near the fire escape.

"What do you have to show me?"

He smelled like a bottle of bourbon; he often fell into drinking when things got tough.

"It's in my car."

"No, I am not leaving with you, Corbin. You know what happened last time."

Corbin's cheeks turned red. "Giselle, please, Bosco is lying to you. Jason loved you and he didn't steal money."

"No matter what he did, Jason is dead because of you." I took inventory of his demeanor. Corbin for many years made me feel beneath him and his family.

The shift in his eyes let me know that something was off. "I am trying to make you understand Bosco is lying. There was never any theft. I can prove it."

"Show me the proof," I forced his hand.

"In my car."

I shifted and looked back at the crowd. I felt safe enough; they would be able to see me if something went wrong. "Let me check with my friends first so they know where I am."

Corbin patted me on the back. "Invite them with you."

A dark plague seemed to follow Corbin, especially with him losing money from gambling. The business sector wanted nothing to do with him.

"What?"

"If it makes you feel better, have them come with you."

I peered into his eyes and down to my phone to see a text from Rena.

Rena: *Champagne is being passed around.*

Me: *Come to the back room near the fire exit.*

Rena: *Are you all right?*

Me: *Fine. I want to show you something.*

Rena: *Mckayla and I are coming.*

I held up my phone. "Rena and Mckayla are my friends. If you try to hurt them, then I will call the police."

The fashion show music changed, and the lights dimmed for the tonal change of the next dresses.

"Promise you, all your questions will be answered." Corbin gave a wry smile.

I jumped when I felt a hand on my shoulder and saw Rena frowning. I leaned close and placed my arms around her to give her a hug.

"Sorry to pull you from the event, I want you to meet Jason's father. Corbin Ford," I introduced.

"Hello." Rena peered at him.

Mckayla glared and I felt bad bringing them into my drama.

Corbin escorted us downstairs, shoved the exit door open, and I saw cars driving up and down the block.

"What do you have to show me, Corbin?"

"This." Corbin held up his phone and I went to grab it when it dropped out of his hand. A white cloth covered my face.

"Hey!" Rena yelled.

I tried to fight Corbin off, but a white van pulled up in front of us, and a group of men jumped out and snatched me up, along with Rena and Mckayla. Within minutes, I felt sluggish. My eyes grew heavy until everything went black.

"Let go!" someone yelled just before I passed out.

* * *

Slowly I flickered my eyes open. I felt stiff in my joints. I held up my hands and saw a bracelet wrapped around my wrist. "Two. Four. Nine," I read the numbers.

"Giselle!" a voice whispered.

I turned to the left, then right, and noticed I was in a room alone. "Hello?"

A loud bang on the wall startled me. "Giselle, it's Rena."

"Rena," I muttered, then leaned my head on the wall to hear her voice.

"Yes, we need to get out of here."

"Where are you?" I stood from the cot—dazed still from earlier—stumbled up to the wall, and touched around to see if I could find a light.

A sob rose in her throat. "We've been *kidnapped*."

Devasted at what I let happen, anger and tears filled my body. "Oh, no! He promised me."

"Corbin lied to you. Some type of sex trafficking bullshit."

I stroked my hand through my ruffled hair. "Bosco."

"You've been sleeping for a few hours."

Still slow in my movements, I checked down at my feet and hands to see I was still dressed. "Rena, where's Mckayla?"

"I'm here, Giselle," Mckayla responded.

"Shut the fuck up!" a deep sinister voice shouted. He came closer and banged on the door.

The locks turned and he stepped in front of me with two men behind him. "She's going to go for a nice price."

113

"Where's Corbin?" I demanded.

"Bring her out." He dismissed my question and turned away from me.

"Corbin!" I shouted. I raised a hand and slapped one of his guys across the face as he tried to push me forward.

"Let her go!" Rena screamed as Mckayla was being pulled toward the opposite direction.

"Steele wants you two up front, he's sold the other bitch off," he explained.

"Do you know who the hell you've taken?" Rena fussed.

I searched around the dark hallway. Rena was nudged closer to me, and I grabbed her hand, so we could stick close together. "Let me speak to Steele."

He chuckled. "Bitch you don't get to demand anything." He shoved us forward. "Now walk."

I looked around at the damp walls. Some cries came from other rooms.

"There's more girls here," Rena said.

Corbin had done the most disgusting shit to me in the past, but selling women for money hit a new low—even for him. *Did Jason know this about his father?*

"Get in there." The guy pushed us forward.

I hesitated and looked over at Rena. She nodded to go forward. I marched upstairs and pushed the curtains back with my mouth agape.

A room full of men sat at tables, some older and a few near my age.

"What is this?"

"Gentlemen, we have two lovely women who are ready to be taken for service," a gravelly voice said.

I scanned the room and none of the men held a microphone. I stared up to the ceilings and saw a speaker.

"My husband's going to kill each and every one of you!"

Rena screamed, turning to the guy who brought us out of the dungeon and punching him in the stomach.

"Grab her!" the fat one shouted.

The guy over the speaker laughed. "Both women are a part of the Calabresi cartel. The bidding will start at one million dollars."

"One-five," said a man in a bow tie, with short, curly hair, a mustache, and a mole on his right cheek.

"Two million." Another bid.

I froze at his comment and shook my head. "No! let her go."

Another guard laced a collar around my neck, and I pushed his hand away and kicked him in the balls.

"Rena, run!" I charged at the other guard and lunged at him. A few of the guys from the audience started to run, and I heard a loud blast.

"It's the Calabresi!"

I rushed to climb downstairs. "Bosco!"

"Take her through the tunnels!" he shouted, and they dragged me and Rena away.

Rattta! Rattta!

One of the men who tried to buy us fell to the ground. Rena kicked another one in the chest, and she was pushed to the ground.

The back gate opened and a man I hadn't seen before stood with a gun in his hand.

"Giselle Ford, nice to meet you, sexy."

"Bosco is going to kill you."

He palmed my chin. "My name is Steele Graziano, your little boyfriend can't handle me," he whispered and brushed a hair behind my ear.

Pop! Pop!

The guard who held me was shot in the back, and I fell

to the ground and crawled away. I snatched his gun and turned to shoot. Steele was gone. I focused on Rena and Mckayla, then stood and ran back inside.

Armani waved at me. "Gigi!"

"Armani, they have Mckayla and Rena." I rushed toward him.

"Come on, we have to get you outside."

I paused as panic ran through my body. "There are more girls. We can't leave."

"Bosco is going crazy. We have to get you out of here." Armani directed a few of their men to cover the back and front entrances.

I tried to move out of his grip, but he nudged me back to leave. "Where is he?"

"Arghhh!" A loud scream blasted off from someone.

I gripped his arm, frozen in place as silence filled the hall.

"That's Bosco taking care of business, come on," Armani informed.

"No, I want to help, and it's all my fault." I sprinted back through the curtains and down the steps to the tunnels where I saw some girls being removed.

Armani and I never really had a conversation, but to see how he jumped in to help me and look after his brother showed he wasn't asshole like his older brother.

Bosco came up beside me, tucked a hand under my chin, turned my face left to right. "Giselle, you shouldn't be here."

"Corbin set me up," I told him.

"We know, go back upstairs with Armani." Bosco pushed me forward.

"Where's Mckayla and Rena?"

"Right here." Rena held on to Mckayla and limped out. Savio picked Mckayla up and carried her in his arms.

I wrapped an arm around her, stepped back, and caught Savio with a glare. "Mckayla."

"Give him a moment," Rena said.

"I-I... didn't mean for this to happen," I stammered.

"He will calm down. Give him some time," Giosuè explained, guiding more young girls from the back.

"Arghhhh! Please no!" a man yelled.

Armani turned me away, escorted me back outside, and waited in the back of the car. Nero handed me a bottle of water, and I thanked him. Rena and Mckayla were placed in separate cars. They had a fleet lined up, ready for war. I dragged a hand down my face; I was hurt that I'd gotten them involved in my situation. If Corbin were there in front of me, I would have killed him myself.

Startled by the door being jerked open, I stared at Bosco, who had blood all over his body, clothes, and hands.

"Bosco—"

A shadow over his face. "Did they touch you?"

"No."

"Good, Nero and Keith are going to take you home."

"Corbin." I wanted him dead.

"We'll talk later, I have to make sure everything is cleaned up here." Bosco slammed the door closed.

I watched him walk over to the car where Savio placed Mckayla. They were in a heated argument. Sante whispered in Savio's ear. Bosco and Savio hugged, and he stalked over to the old, abandoned building. There were no signs or a clear address on the building to give the police any type of location where they could come and arrest the people who held us hostage. If I was being honest, Bosco saved me. He was my very own hero who stopped at nothing to get me back safely.

I leaned back in the seat, closed my eyes, and sighed, then popped up to see Nero and Keith hopping in and starting the engine.

"Keith—"

This was my only chance to apologize, if Keith allowed, but the awkwardness in the air seemed to speak for itself.

Keith turned in his seat. "Bosco is a friend. I take my job seriously, Giselle."

I gulped down the dryness. "I get it."

"Normally, something like this would have him killed for letting you be taken twice," Nero chimed in to reiterate.

"I understand."

Nero put the car in drive and slid behind another car. All I could think about was how much I'd put everybody in danger thanks to my recklessness with Corbin.

* * *

The house was quiet, Yun cooked for me and said she'd leave it in the kitchen. I came out wearing a robe and my hair tied up in a bun. A few men stood near the front door, at the rear of the house that led to the backyard with their eyes avoiding me.

I lifted the top off the pot on the stove and smelled the stew. I picked up the spoon and bowl, then filled it up and added a piece of cornbread. The alarm chirped, and I stiffened, ready for Bosco to come in and yell at me.

I placed the bowl on the table and sat.

Bosco walked right by me without saying a word.

I dropped the spoon in the bowl, rose from the stool,

took a napkin from the counter, and heard the door chime again.

She laid her bag on the back of the stool. "Hey." Rena ran toward me.

"Rena, how is Mckayla?"

"I'm fine." Mckayla walked in behind her.

Tears filled my eyes, and I dabbed them away with my napkin, then wrapped my arms around her neck. My thoughts swam around me, remembering the warped events of almost being sold. I couldn't fault them if they blamed me and wanted to push me away.

"I am so sorry."

"Hush, don't worry. We are used to chaos," Mckayla tittered.

I was recognizing all my mistakes. Even with everything Jason caused, I was no better. "Savio hates me."

"He only hates you a little bit," Rena joked, and Mckayla slapped her on the arm.

I covered my face with both hands and groaned. "Oh, my God."

Mckayla pulled my hands down and wiped tears from my cheek. "He will be fine. We talked."

"She promised to give him something later if he stopped being mad," Rena teased and wiggled her brows.

"Shut up, Rena." Mckayla cackled and smacked her on the butt.

Rena and I laughed at her joke.

A hiccup formed and I held my breath for a second. "Bosco hasn't talked to me yet."

Rena ambled to the sink, removed a cup from the cabinet, and turned on the faucet. She handed it to me to drink. "Give him some space, he was scared."

"How do you know?"

"The men act like they're big bad bullies, but really they're sweet and sensitive."

"Have you eaten yet?" I turned to the stove and gestured to the pot of stew.

"Giselle." Bosco entered the kitchen.

Mckayla and Rena started to fill a bowl of stew each, then nodded for me to talk to him.

Bosco turned and motioned for me to follow him. I strode out of the kitchen and trailed him to the theater room. Bosco sat on the couch, then lifted the remote to the screen. "Shut the door." His muscles bulged noticeably through his T-shirt, and I admired his rounded shoulders and long fingers.

"I'm sorry," I blurted out.

"He could have hurt you today, belladonna."

I fidgeted my hands. "You care."

"If I wanted you dead, you would have been gone a long time ago. The shit you keep pulling makes my men look at me differently."

"I thought I could see Corbin and get the truth from him."

"Corbin wants you dead."

I hugged myself, reeling in my anxiety. "I know that now. You wouldn't understand." One of my terrible traits is being obsessively devoted to finding the truth.

"It's all about Jason," he grunted.

"Yes! My husband was killed by you," I hissed and set my chin in a stubborn line, anger boiled in my chest.

After chugging the drink, he walked up to me, grasped me by my neck, and squeezed. "Jason stole money, and I killed him. That's my job." His expression was one of bitter jealousy. "He was worthless. The dirt on my shoe is more important. You want me to say sorry?"

I jerked out of his grip. "I want you to understand what happened four years ago hurt me. I know what Jason did was wrong, but he was all I had."

"Get over it." Bosco scoffed, flapping his hand in the air.

I shoved him in the chest, then smacked him in the face. "I have! You don't care is the problem." I burst into tears.

Bosco's sneer slowly fell, and he caressed my cheek. I tried to move out of his grip, but he held onto me tighter.

Something in that moment changed, he drew in closer and without hesitation, our lips locked onto each other at a familiar pace.

"Mmmmhhh." I moaned and locked my hands around his neck.

Bosco stroked a hand up my back and growled. "*Giselle*." A soft groan filled my ears.

"Yes," I whimpered, placing both hands on his chest.

Bosco held his forehead on mine. "You want to go to dinner?"

I giggled and opened my eyes. "Dinner?"

He cleared his throat. "We haven't done the conventional route, so I think dinner as a first date would be good."

"The money."

Heat built up at the feel of his hands kneading my thigh.

I know it was wrong to like the touch of the man that killed my husband, but I couldn't walk away from him.

"Steele and Corbin will die, right along with Allen, for touching you."

"I want to be there when you kill Corbin."

My statement had his brows furrowed. "You've seen enough."

"Bosco stop trying to keep me locked away, all the girls

know what is happening. Savio—" I paused at his name, and my eyes rose in thought.

"I need to talk to Savio."

"Savio's not the most rational at the moment."

I ran a finger across Bosco's lips.

He kissed the back of my hand, his mouth curved into a smile.

I drew back. I wanted to be back in his arms, but I was locked down from all the chaos. "The girls. I left them alone in the kitchen."

Bosco ran a hand over my back. "Hurry up and get rid of them. I want to spend some time with you before I go to the club."

"Always working."

"I'm the underboss of the cartel. I have to make an example out of a few people."

"Can you promise to let me be there when you kill Corbin?" A stab of guilt stung my heart.

"I promise, Gigi."

I ambled down the hall back to the kitchen, Rena smirked at me.

"She's going to kick us to the curb," Rena jested.

"Sorry, ladies."

"We understand," Mckayla spoke.

"Please enjoy the food." I hugged them and walked away as they teased us. The softness Bosco extended was rare, and I appreciated that he let me in however it made him look. I shut the door behind me. "Thank you, I have to call my family and check in after today."

"I will be late coming in tonight."

"Like the other night?"

"The less you know the better."

After he filled his glass again, we sat back down on the couch and turned on a movie.

Chapter Ten

Bosco

Giselle and I fell into a routine of having dinner together, breakfast in the morning, and lunch from time to time. We hadn't taken it to the next level, but we'd come close a few times, eye-fucking and flirting when we were alone. Even though she hadn't had sex in few years, I respected her pace of doing things slow after the incident with Steele and Corbin trying to sell her to human traffickers. I put a bounty out on the streets. I wanted them alive and brought to me for one million dollars.

I'd agreed to dinner later today once I finished work.

I came to a stop at one of my old stomping grounds in Jersey. It was the turf of the Thunder biker gang, a longtime friend to me and my family. Their leader, Lake, taught me about bikes and bailed me out of a few situations that my brother had no clue about. I swung my leg off my bike and slapped hands with Billy and Roger, Lake's second-and-third-in-command.

I pointed with my chin in greeting at some of the other guys stationed outside the bar, then ran a hand across the top seat of the Red Devil that belonged to Lake.

"Money Man Bosco, we never catch you here with the little guys," Roger jested, clapping me on the shoulder.

I pushed his hand off my shoulder. "Roger, you know as well as me that the Thunder biker gang is very wealthy. I should ask you about some money."

Roger chuckled and crossed his arms. "Heard you have some problems with Grazianos."

"Titus's nephew touched something that doesn't belong to them."

Billy's brow cocked high. "He's into some weird business."

"That's why I came to visit and find out what you guys know."

"I had a few run-ins with them a few months back, tried to sell some drugs in our bar and a few girls said a few of his men tried to pick them up." Lake held the door open to the bar.

I pushed off the railing, marched inside, and slapped hands with a few Thunder bikers drinking at the bar.

Lake flicked a hand to the bartender to pour me a shot and refill his glass.

I drank the bourbon down, and motioned for another one, then slid a hand in my pocket and grabbed my wallet.

Lake pushed my hand away. "Your money's not good here."

Roger and Billy came up to the bar and ordered a round for the entire room and sat down.

"Steele is working with Allen to bring my family down."

Lake picked up a few peanuts from the bowl, tossing them in his mouth.

"He sent out a few subliminal threats. I had to knock

him on his ass the other day." Roger clinked glasses with Lake.

Lake shoved his hand in his pockets, leaning against the bar. "Tomorrow, we're going for a ride. You should try to hang with us."

The shouting voices of a few men playing cards got louder in the near corner.

Some Thunder members got angry. Lake jumped in the middle to break up the fight, and I chuckled at Billy when he smacked Simon in the back of the head.

"Stop stealing, Simon," Lake argued, snatching the money from his hand and handing it to Arnold.

"Two beers," Lake told me, and I held a hand up to stop the bartender.

"I have to get back to the city, I have dinner plans."

"Dinner plans? You and a woman?" Billy jested.

Roger snatched the beer from Lake. "What's her name?"

"None of your business."

They laughed and knew I would keep secrets if she was special to me.

I marched to the door and tugged on the handle. "Next time, fellas." I saluted Roger and Billy as they laughed. I turned to remove my keys from my pocket when I froze at a bike creeping slowly down the street with a gun pointed in my direction. It felt like a movie in slow motion as I dropped my keys, my eyes bugged wide. Lake frowned in confusion and scanned outside the window as bullets started to go through the windows.

"Get down!"

Pop! Pop!

"I need a gun!" I yelled, stretched my hand toward him.

Roger reached behind the bar, passed me a shotgun, and lifted his gun from his holster.

I raised the shotgun and sent two shots back to the car behind the bike.

"Billy, watch out!"

The windows shattered, and shotgun shells passed back and forth.

Ignoring Lake's commands, Roger rushed outside and hopped on his bike without a care for his safety.

"He's going to get himself killed," Lake fussed.

I jumped up from the floor, ran after him, stuck my helmet on, started my bike, and drove up next to Roger.

"Take the car on the left," I demanded.

Billy and the rest of the Thunder bikers joined us.

The car eased through traffic, knocked the back window out, and started shooting. I swiveled around to the back buildings and sped up as people moved to get out of the way.

"Take him on the right. I want their heads, try and keep one alive." I pushed the gas, swerved back to the main road and cut the car off, then held up the shotgun and sent a bullet through the driver's side. He whirled to the side and crashed into the light pole.

"Call the police!" someone shouted.

A few people removed their phones and started filming and pointed at me.

"Shit, we have to go." I revved the engine and drove away to catch up to the first shooter that was heading for the freeway.

Lake pulled up alongside me and signaled that he would move to my right side.

I watched him start to cut off a driver and sent a few bullets past the shooter, and I felt my phone go off and heard a horn. I glanced to my left to see Armani in his car chuck his chin up in acknowledgement and go in front of me as a decoy. I hung on the side of his car as traffic slowed down to get off the exit and raised the shotgun.

The driver caught wind of Lake, then Armani. He shot at us, blasted the tires out of a car behind us, and sped away.

* * *

Not ready to deal with the police, I made it back home and jumped in the shower to change my clothes. Giselle left a note that she was leaving work to head straight to her parents' house for dinner. It would be the first time we would all be together since I brought her to my home.

I jogged downstairs and stepped in my office to greet Armani and Giosuè, who were drinking and talking on the loudspeaker.

Giosuè stood in front of me, wrapped a hand on the back of my neck, and pointed his finger in my face, trying to get my eyes to follow his fingertip as he moved it back and forth. "You hurt?"

I knocked his hand down and walked around to my desk. "No, just pissed he got away."

"Aaron sent word the bodies of the men in the car are DOA," Armani replied.

Giosuè sat on the edge of the couch.

"Giselle wants me at dinner; I can't go until later or tomorrow."

"He's becoming like you," Armani teased.

Giosuè shrugged and ignored my brother.

"Giselle is different."

"I said the same about Penelope," Giosuè jested.

My brothers knew me and how my dating life is me

128

hooking up with women, then moving on. "We haven't had had sex yet," I confessed.

Giosuè choked on his drink. "Hold up, my little brother Bosco Calabresi hasn't bagged the girl that's staying at his house?" Giosuè jerked his head from left to right.

I slouched down on the couch next to him. "She's not a girl who I would fuck and drop off."

"Dinner with the family is a big deal." Giosuè's steely gaze bore into my face.

"I know the reason we took her was because of Jason, but she's become more than an enemy."

Armani scrunched his brows and titled his head the side. "Make sure you don't become stupid over this girl."

I cocked my head to stare at him. "Did I run your love life with Penelope?"

Armani kicked me in the leg, and Giosuè peered at us.

"Watch your mouth. Armani knows, like me, you've been the biggest whore out the three of us. If anything, look out for her best interest."

"Lock up when you leave and keep me updated if you find Allen or Steele."

* * *

Giselle placed the mashed potatoes on the table and kissed her mother on the cheek. I sat and scrolled through my phone, looking at the text thread between Armani, Giosuè, Lake, and Savio discussing today's events.

Armani: *We got Allen at the warehouse.*
Me: *Where did you find him?*
Savio: *I got the footage from Lake's bar.*
Lake: *We have cameras for situations that come up.*
Me: *Keep him on ice.*

L.K. Ryan

Giosuè*: The shooting is online.*

I bit my lip and hung my head at more drama with the media. "Shit."

"Bosco, where do you work again?" Mallory investigated and sat at the table with a wide smirk.

I sighed and tucked the cell back in my pocket. Giselle rolled her eyes at Mallory. I understand siblings wanted to protect each other, but I could tell her sister couldn't stand me and the feeling was mutual.

"Mallory, you promised to be nice tonight," Giselle said.

Mallory's cocky demeanor oozed through her grin. She scooped up the vegetables and turkey. "Does Mom and Dad know your boyfriend threatened you?" She pointed the fork at her.

Aaron came back to the dining room table from the backyard and sat down at the head of the table.

"Mallory's always been protective of Giselle." Her mom pulled out a chair. "Mr. Calabresi tell me about yourself," Giselle's mom, Maura, probed.

"I run a trucking business and my family's background started from the oil business. But I mostly focus on the club and trucking company."

"He's a gangster, Mom. I see the men that hang around him, they even threatened Giselle and me," her sister hurriedly jumped in to tell my business.

"Mallory! Please," Giselle groaned.

I stretched a hand across the table to cover Giselle's palm. "Mallory is correct, our family has ties to some things that would be considered in the underworld."

The prickle of sweat poured down her forehead, and she slammed her hand on the table. "He's a killer!" Mallory spat.

Maura looked at Giselle, then her husband, and jumped up to rush out of the dining room.

Giselle ran after her. "Mom."

"Dad, you should have him arrested!" Mallory's loud voice rumbled off the cream-painted walls. Deep lines creased her forehead.

"If that's the case, then your dad will go down with me," I responded snarkily.

Mallory dropped the snarl and stared at her father for answers. "Dad," she muttered.

"Mallory, I know their family because I crossed paths with them during some policework," Aaron told her.

Mallory tossed her napkin on the table and jumped up from the table and lunged at me with her hands in the air.

"I want you out of here!" Mallory shouted.

Aaron stepped closer. "Mallory!"Aaron barked and moved to block her from me.

I smirked at her.

Giselle and her mom sauntered back into the dining room with perplexed looks.

"Giselle, if you continue to stay with him, then you are dead to this family," Mallory announced, snatching herself out of her father's hold and marching to the kitchen. No one could convince me that her mind wasn't narrow, repetitive, or vapid. Her husband probably allowed her to run the household to keep the peace.

Her mom and dad went to check on Mallory and left us alone.

Giselle leaned her head on my chest. "I'm sorry about my sister." She sighed and caressed a hand on my cheek.

I kissed the top of her head and lifted my ringing phone. "Armani," I answered.

"We got a location on Steele," Armani explained.

Giselle looked at me, her parents walked back in holding hands.

"Let me call you back."

"Meet us at the cabin." Armani hung up.

She pulled back, sliding her hands off my chest. "You're leaving."

I kissed her on the cheek. "I have Keith and Mikell outside for when you're ready to leave."

"Giselle, we need to talk," Maura stated.

My hatred for her sister was a living thing. I couldn't fake happy.

"I will be home when you're ready."

"Bosco—"

I rubbed her shoulder and pecked her on the lips. "Don't worry, I will be back. Nothing will stop me." I nodded at her mother and father, then left her family's home.

Keith and Mikell laughed together and straightened when I came closer and climbed in my Range Rover.

"Her sister's a little pissed off, watch her, but make sure Giselle comes home."

"If she forces her to stay?"

"Aaron won't allow it if he knows what's good for him." The ignition started and I flipped on the lights.

The front door opened, and Giselle ran out to the car and opened the driver's side door.

"I want to go with you."

"What about dinner with your parents?"

"We can reschedule and besides my sister is going on a tangent and Dad is trying to calm my mom down."

"Mallory's really going to be a problem, I need you to understand she is never welcome in my space."

"I will talk to her, but I know you're going to find somebody."

"We got a hit on Allen."

"I want to go and before you say no, it was me that he tried to kill."

"Giselle, it can get dangerous."

"I can handle myself." She ran around to the other side, climbed in, and pressed a kiss on my lips.

Keith and Mikell hopped in the Lincoln town car.

Giselle locked in her seatbelt, her citrus and lemon floral scent hit my nose. I was running out of time and wanted to take her back home and lock us away for days learning all her special points. Allen's death was too close to let go.

"If it becomes too much tonight, then you will go home with Keith and Mikell. Understand me?"

Giselle laid her head back on the seat. "I understand, and honestly since Jason's death nothing really shocks me anymore."

Chapter Eleven

Giselle

Bosco helped me out of the truck, and Keith trailed us. I nodded at him to let him know that I was fine as we walked into the cabin. On the ride over, Bosco explained about the warehouse being shot up, and how they were moving to a new place. In the meantime, they were using the cabin in the woods. Armani popped out and waved him inside. He wore black gloves and a mask, and he motioned for Bosco to pick up a pair on the table.

"Put these on," Bosco said.

I cupped my mouth at the sight of Allen sitting naked in a chair, the smell in the room showed he had been here for a few hours from the feces and blood mixed together.

"He's not talking." Armani ushered me to stand in the back corner. I watched Bosco go in the front of the cabin and whisper something to Allen. Whatever it was Allen's eyes widened in fear.

"Giselle." Savio stepped in front of me, and I backed up, nervous about him coming at me. A silver streak of hair framed his dark brown curls. Mckayla was a lucky woman.

"Savio."

"Mckayla told me to apologize." A cold, hard, pinched expression engulfed his face.

"She did?"

Savio ran a hand down his neck. "I won't apologize for protecting my wife."

"I agree."

His voice brimmed with distaste. "She shouldn't have been in that situation, but it wasn't your fault.

"Arghhh!" Allen shouted.

"Mckayla and Rena are special women."

"Where the fuck is Steele and Corbin?" Bosco barked.

"I don't know," Allen cried.

Savio turned to face Allen. "He knows he's going to die tonight. Once Bosco turns into the machine of a killer, everyone starts to confess."

"Am I crazy for wanting to be with him even though he killed my husband?"

The smell of sweat, piss, and blood wafted in the air.

"Did Mckayla tell you how we met?"

Savio had political talent, natural charm, and the gift of persuasion.

"She wrote a story on your dad."

"It's not just the story. She saw something that she shouldn't have. Mckayla is my lifeline, and I know Bosco took a while to show his feelings, but I know from the way we almost fought that he cares about you a lot."

Allen interrupted, "I gave them the tracking routes of the drops at your trucking business."

"Son of a bitch!" Giosuè yelled.

Bosco lifted a bow and arrow in his hand, then walked back to the cabin's wall.

"Bosco, wait, we can talk about how we can work together," Allen pleaded.

"Stop begging. You snitching tells me I can't trust you."

"She's not safe!" Allen shouted.

Bosco paused and glanced at me. I walked forward and Savio grabbed my hand to stop me.

"Stay there, Giselle."

Allen sneered and spit on the ground. "Steele's not the only one looking for you Giselle, Corbin wanted to help you before it was too late."

"Help me how? Trying to sell me away."

Allen chuckled. "Pussy pays, what can we say? The money would have gone toward the debt."

"You are a dead man Allen, so keep talking," Giosuè grunted.

"How did he know about the Thunder bikers bar? Are they following me?"

Allen nodded at me. "Her phone is tapped, and they found out where you'd be," Allen confessed. "They hacked into your trucking company's routes. They're going to come after you."

My shoulders tensed. "You are evil," I muttered as my neck grew hot.

"Where's your phone?" Bosco questioned.

"At my parents' house."

"Make sure that someone's watching her parents' house," Bosco told Keith, who rushed to leave the cabin.

"Anything else you want to confess before you die?"

"Your husband and sister." Allen's breathing slowed down.

I crossed my arms. "Excuse me."

"I knew your husband and he was dating Mallory, and she's the reason you became a witness that night." Allen grinned through bloody teeth.

"Mallory?" I whispered.

"She threatened him with the affair, and he tried to break it off, but she wanted money instead."

"You're a liar!"

Allen gestured to his bloodied body. "I have no reason to lie anymore. Bosco's going to kill me anyway. Jason and Corbin helped get me a piece of the Calabresi money, and I used that to work my way in with them to buy product."

"So, you bought product with our own money," Bosco remarked.

Allen nodded in agreement.

"What did Corbin and Jason get out of this arrangement?" Giosuè wondered.

As he continued to talk, he twitched. "Money—but he dipped into it a little too much when Mallory got greedy."

I held a hand to my rumbling stomach, and nausea rose to my throat. "I think I'm going to be sick."

"Armani follow her to the bathroom," Bosco demanded.

I busted through the bathroom door, fell to my knees in front of the toilet, and threw up the lunch I had earlier.

"Ughhhh!" Allen screamed.

With shaky fingers, I looked up at Armani for some type of support. "Mallory lied to me." I sat back on my legs and wiped tears from my eyes.

"Do you need anything?"

"I need to think."

"Come on, Bosco's probably looking for you." Armani bent down to help me stand, and I moved closer to the sink and washed my face and stared into the mirror.

"She slept with my husband."

"We have to go."

"Is he going to kill her?"

Armani ignored my question. "I have to get you out of here and back home, cleaning crew is coming."

The living room was filled with about six extra men, all of them wearing white suits. They had removed Allen's body from the chair. Bosco killed him with about four arrows in his chest, arm, and leg.

Bosco directed orders to Mikell and a few of his men near his car. I waited near the side of his car. Armani came up to them and gestured to me. He finished their conversation, approached the car, and held the door open for me. I slid in, and he slammed it shut. I wondered if he was angry with me, and whether he would possibly hurt my family after Allen's interrogation. I stared out the window as we left the cabin at the bodies being walked to the back of the van.

* * *

Since the cabin, it had been hard to return to a normal routine and not replay the events. Bosco worked hard to put me at ease, and we'd gone on more little dates. He'd even tried to cook, but Yun mostly prepared the meals. We'd gotten closer and talked more about ourselves.

Bosco had come to the fashion show tonight, and his support was shocking. Rena, Mckayla, and their husbands rode along with them and sat near me in the front row.

My story was sitting on my computer, ready to be published tonight, but Bosco had offered to let me enjoy his sauna, which he usually used after a long workout. The torment of his presence challenged me, and interest radiated from the depths of his dark eyes.

I thought Jason had been the biggest size I had ever seen, but now that I was staring at Bosco's dick in front of my face, I knew it had to be at least nine inches. I gulped down the nervousness in my throat and sat up on the bench in the sauna with my towel wrapped securely over my body.

"You are the most beautiful woman I've ever met."

I could tell he wanted to unleash, and my heart reacted immediately to his touch.

"Thank you."

"Allen, Steele, and Corbin will pay for trying to hurt you." A touch triggered primitive yearnings.

I blinked back at his words and lifted my hands to his arms.

Bosco cupped my chin and rubbed his finger across my lower lips. I submissively parted them open, and he stuck his thumb in and out. I closed my lips and sucked him in and out through a moan. Bosco smirked and pulled his finger away, then brushed the back of his palm across my chest, undid the towel, and let it fall to the ground.

When he tweaked my nipple a light smirk toiled at his lips. "Sexy Gigi."

"Bosco," I cooed, arching my back into his grip.

A kiss full of passion and need, his hold tightened around me. "You're officially mine, you understand?"

I nodded in answer and watched him drop to his knees. He pulled my legs apart, kissed up my thigh to my center, and pressed a kiss to my pussy.

I panted, clenched him by both shoulders, and picked my legs up to give him more space. "Bosco....ummhmmm..." All of me embraced him, breathless and urgent. A small sound of wonder came from my throat.

The warmth of his mouth was demanding. "Fuck, you taste like I predicted, baby."

"Bosco! Oh, God!"

I must have been extremely lightweight to him because he picked me up and threw me over his shoulder, then turned around and lay down on the bench with me on top. I rolled my hips, and he took both sides of my ass and squeezed tightly. I sucked in a deep breath, felt him smack my ass, and tried to hold onto the wall when he suddenly slipped a hand up my stomach to my breasts.

"Shit! Right there, Bosco."

I felt dizziness as his tongue sucked onto my clit, flutters filled my belly, and my eyes were squeezed closed. Shooting stars blasted off and goosebumps rose up my arm.

Bosco finally released his hold and eased me onto his thick erection. My mouth fell open at the feeling of him.

His jaw clenched, and his gaze found mine. He leaned up and nuzzled his face against my neck. "Gigi... shit, baby." The pressure of his hands and the firmness of his body gave me comfort.

I slowly rocked back and forth. I never knew how good it could feel when you let go of any restraints or judgement. I felt the touch of Bosco's calloused hands against mine. He smashed his lips on top of mine and sucked my tongue.

"We need the bed, not enough room," Bosco grunted and lifted me up, still in his hold.

"Bosco!" I screeched from the pressure of his fast movements.

He pushed me against the back of the elevator, still pumping in and out of my pussy slowly.

"Press the button to second floor," he demanded.

I stretched my hand over his shoulder, the fires within me burned at how he carved into my heart.

Seconds later, we made it to the first bedroom. He placed me on top of the bed. I reached over my head and looked out of the corner of my eye to see handcuffs.

"Bosco," I panted, my chest heaving up and down.

"I can make you my full course meal, if you let me."

I bit my bottom lip, waited as he spread my legs wide open, sucked on my neck, moved down to my breasts and cupped each one.

I watched him push two fingers in, moving faster and faster, then flatten his tongue, sending me on a wild ride. I tried to close my legs, push him back, too much pressure caused my head to spin and my heart rate to rise high.

Bosco gripped the back of my hair, sucking along my shoulder to my neck and pulling my earlobe into his mouth. He gently bit me, pumping faster and faster. The sounds of our bodies clapping together filled the bedroom. My body convulsed, and stars filled my eyes. I tried to get out of the tight cuffs. My breath hitched, and I arched off the bed.

"Bosco, pleassseee..." I begged; the heavy ache of his male hunger drowned me.

"Fuck, yes... Gigi, take it, baby. You take it so good."

He devoured my breasts. His hands tightened around my throat, and everything in me wanted to stay in this room with him forever.

"Yessss! Oh, God," I panted, letting my dormant sexuality be awakened.

"Look at your pretty pussy being filled up, next time you can taste me first. Come for me, baby."

I shivered under his command, and our fluids combined. He stiffened, threw his head back, and closed his eyes.

"Damn, I want to wake up to you like this tomorrow, tied up at my command." Bosco grinned, leaned over, released my hands, climbed out of bed, and walked to the bathroom. Seconds later, he came back with a warm towel and cleaned me up, then cleaned himself. He rubbed the soreness from my wrists and lifted me up.

"Where are we going?" I yawned.

"To my bedroom, I will clean the sheets in the morning."

The lights turned off in the bedroom, and I turned them back on and slid up close to the headboard. He frowned.

Even after our sex, I was more excited to cuddle. "We have to talk."

"Nothing to talk about."

"My sister and husband stole from you and had an affair."

Bosco sat on the edge of bed with his back to me. "Do you still care about him?"

"No, my feelings for Jason disappeared years ago. I missed what we had in the beginning, but after learning what he's done, I could never see myself with a person like that."

"Like me." Bosco's naked chest molded into me.

"I know what you've done Bosco, it wasn't out of malice, and Mallory could have come to me years ago, but she lied."

"My brother thinks I should kill your sister."

At his statement I tried to sit up, but he held me down. "What did you tell him?" I was haunted to think how Jason's decision would destroy Mallory.

"I said I couldn't do that to you after everything with your ex."

"I know it's stupid to want to keep her safe, but she's my sister; she was my best friend growing up. I know my parents would hate me if they found out how she betrayed me."

Bosco pecked me on the top of the head. "Corbin must have gotten your whereabouts from Mallory, she had to know more."

"I'm going to talk to her tomorrow."

"I don't want you over there anymore."

I sucked my teeth. "Bosco, it's my parents."

"So far Mallory was having an affair, and your husband stole money and left you to die."

I sat forward, extended my arms around his neck, and kissed the side of his cheek. "Let me talk to her first and see what she says."

Bosco cupped my thigh and turned his head to kiss me on the lips.

I slid my hand down his chest. "Let's go to sleep; I want to forget about my family for the night."

He growled and turned me to push me on my back. "Your scent drives me crazy."

"I belong here with you."

The outside world knew him as a cold killer and an underboss, but with me, he let his heart be open. The many textures and layers of growth in how he had treated me since I first came to know him made me fall even harder for him. This underboss exuded strength, longing, and passion to make sure that I was protected.

Chapter Twelve

Bosco

When I heard how hurt Giselle had been by her sister and late husband, my pulse increased, and fire engulfed my insides, while the taste of revenge sat in my heart. I now understood her hesitation to be with me, but I replaced the pain in her eyes with the sweet moans of our lovemaking.

At first, I hesitated when she argued about wanting to be back at work. From what I gathered, her boss had agreed to let her come back—as long as she focused more on her work. The top bosses felt that she was lacking, but when she explained the kidnapping, they bent the rules to let my guys stand guard at her office as a precaution.

I watched her go into work today, and I decided to get out on the streets and find Steele and Corbin by any means. Giselle's security was the highest priority.

We arrived on Graziano's block to scope out some of his men when they did drops. Armani passed me the binoculars, and I stared at some kids running in the yard of the house next door to the one that sold drugs.

"No movements for the last hour."

I eyed the black Bronco truck backing out of the yard that the kids lived in. The driver honked.

"Allen said they come by here at least twice day."

"I can put some people here; you have work to do at the trucking company."

"Do you think I'm wrong for letting her sister slide?" Since being with my pretty lady, I felt like I was beginning to form a new identity.

"You're the underboss."

I looked at my brother in the driver's seat. "And you're the enforcer."

Armani pulled his gun and sat on his lap. "Put yourself in her shoes, to hear that her sister and husband did the unthinkable has to hurt, more suffering will only turn her against you more."

"When did you become so thoughtful and caring?"

Armani flipped me off.

"I know Giosuè would be the first one to drive by and shoot up her entire family's house."

Armani sighed. His mouth was compressed into a hard line. "I told him I wouldn't do it until he talked to you."

I reared back in shock. "I'm going to kick his ass." I gripped the binoculars.

Armani drew a deep, audible breath. "He's the Don of the family, when decisions are made, we have to understand it's not taken lightly even if we disagree."

"And being our brother, our blood shouldn't be taken into account."

"Right now, Giselle has only made us more involved with her family based on her husband's choices."

"I get it Armani, doing your job."

Armani threw his head back against the seat and

groaned. "If it's worth anything, then I think she's made for you and shouldn't be touched."

"Thanks."

Armani pointed at the cars driving down the block. "They're here."

The bus shook to a stop. The burnt oil smell of machinery wafted in the air. While we stared at the front of the house with the kids playing the doors opened, and a few men stepped out and gave them some money. A few seconds later, Steele Graziano joined them and bent down to talk to the kids.

I cocked my gun and tossed the binoculars in the back seat.

"We're only sending a message."

"If he dies in the middle of bullets, that's on his people for not protecting him."

Buzz Buzz

The loud motorcycle engines got closer, and I looked through the rearview mirror. Lake and some of his guys ran past us and started blasting at Steele.

I slammed my hand on the top of the dashboard. "Shit! Go." My pulse quickened.

Armani sped down the road and leaned out the car window to shoot in their direction.

"Graziano! You're next!"

Pop Pop!

"Down, everyone down," Steele yelled and grabbed a kid and ran back in the house.

"Piece of shit doesn't care about anyone."

The helicopters hovered like vultures in the sky. In a few seconds, the cops would be nearby.

Armani made a U-turn. Lake turned at the same time and paused as his men shot at them.

"Watch the kids!" I barked at Armani. He swerved just in time to miss one that ran in the middle of the street.

Sirens and ambulances appeared closer. We didn't get a chance to do another run of shooting, Steele lived to have another day.

Armani turned onto a side street and followed Lake and the Thunder bikers off the block in the opposite direction. I smacked the side of the door, jumped out of the car, and trailed upstairs to my trucking company.

Lake and Armani shook hands and sat on the couch.

I popped open a beer and paced in front of the window of my office.

Billy handed each one a beer, and I gulped the rest of mine down, then flipped the remote to turn on the TV screen.

"*A biker gang was just shooting at children,*" an older woman on screen said.

Lake turned his nose up in the air. "She got paid off," Lake grumbled.

"Steele's willing to do anything to make us look bad."

Ring

News media had a vested interest in chaos.

"Shit, Giosuè's calling."

Armani took a seat next to Lake. "You better answer him before he calls me."

"I know, Giosuè," I growled.

"Bosco, what the fuck? Children."

Even though he wasn't near, I threw my hands up in the air from the accusations. "That wasn't on us, Steele tried to hide."

"If you saw children out there, then you should have left," Giosuè exploded.

I glanced at Lake. "I know Lake wouldn't have done this if he knew the kids would be used as shields."

"How the fuck can we clean it up? Bad enough her family is moving funny and now this bullshit."

"She's off-limits, Giosuè," I warned him.

"Give me a good reason why?" he challenged.

"Because you've had to make tough decisions that I never agreed to, but I understand as your brother to let it go." There was a kick of fury in the middle of my belly at his threats.

"I want Steele and Corbin dead." He sighed.

I crammed my eyes shut briefly. "I'm working on that right now."

"Work harder."

"Anything else?"

"Savio is thinking of removing us from the inventory of the guns through distribution because of your bullshit."

I pushed a finger through my hair. "Savio is Savio." Everybody let Savio get away with demands, I pretended to agree and did my own thing.

"Our business works because of family loyalty."

Loyalty was tattooed on my chest; Giosuè knew better. "Then I will talk to him myself. I'm not letting her, or her family, get hurt, Giosuè."

"I know and I talked to him."

"What did he say?"

"That if I threatened him again, then I would have to let you make decisions about this situation," Giosuè bellowed.

I smirked at his statement. "I'm at the trucking company watching the news."

"Bosco! Police." Armani snapped his fingers at the security camera.

"Giosuè, I have to go."

"The police are there?" Giosuè inquired.

The lines of my throat twitched at their audacity to come here. "Yeah, send lawyers in case I end up jammed with charges."

"I will call Aaron and see what he knows," Giosuè explained.

"Let him know his older daughter has some secrets." I hit the red button, marched out of my office and to the front lobby of my building and thanked the receptionist.

"Officer, how can I help you?"

"Mr. Calabresi, we have eyewitnesses that saw your vehicle outside a shooting on the freeway and in a residential area."

"Witnesses? We've been here all day working," I taunted with my chin pulled into my chest.

The officer smirked. "Aaron can't save you this time."

"If you look at the cameras, they have us logged in all day."

The officer chucked his head at my brother and friends. "Only you. What about the rest of the Thunder bikers?"

Lake chuckled and started to charge at the police.

"Do it so I can arrest your ass," the officer taunted.

"Nobody's getting arrested today. Whatever Steele is paying you or Ford, I can promise it won't be enough."

A flicker of recognition appeared in his eyes.

Ring

I folded my arms and spread my legs. "I bet that's your captain calling you right now."

"We can search this place, probably have drugs all up and through here," another officer, chimed in and spoke.

"I remember you from arresting my brother a few weeks ago," Armani growled.

I raised a hand in the air to stop him.

"Here." The officer handed me a piece of paper and hung up his phone.

I snatched it from his hands. "A warrant?"

"Betcha! Thought you'd get rid of the drugs early?"

"No drugs here, so if you want to search go ahead." I gestured to the back facility.

"Armani follow him and make sure they clean everything up, if we find anything missing, I promise we'll be filing a lawsuit."

Lake moved closer to me, and I handed him the warrant. "Want us to give them a runaround, have a little fun?"

"No, they're itching to lock you and me up. For now, go look for Steele's slick ass and keep me in the loop."

"Thanks for not giving us up."

"Giosuè talks shit, but he respects my judgement call."

Lake and I did our secret shake, and the rest of the boys left to go back to Jersey.

"Mr. Calabresi, should we cancel the rest of the routes for tonight?" wondered Sherry, my receptionist.

"No, business as usual, don't give them a reason to think we're hiding something."

"Oh, your lawyer has pulled up." Sherry ran to the desk and buzzed him in.

Decklan, our lawyer and longtime family friend, had always been there for my father.

"Decklan, thanks for coming."

"Giosuè called and told me the police are here."

"In the back, I have to finish up some work. Can you handle it your way, before I make it go away?"

Decklan raised his hand. "We have to talk about what happened at the shootout."

"I have a right to protect myself." I grinned, patting him on the back.

* * *

A meeting was called, and I had to leave my business to get there. Sherry and Decklan were left with the police. Giosuè held up the photos of the women we rescued at the location that Giselle was taken. Using my cameras, we made sure that nothing funny was happening. I stared at the video on my phone and watched Decklan talking on his phone, holding the warrant in his hand.

"Obviously, Bosco has a right to make a move since they hurt someone close to him." Giosuè nudged the phone to the middle of the table.

I linked my hands together, leaned close, and stared at each Don that surrounded the table. So far, no one had spoken back or disavowed the situation at Steele's.

"Corbin Ford and Steele are running a sex trafficking business in our city."

I dragged my eyes from Marcheline. "As far as we know it was one location on the East side, near your territory Marcheline."

"The fuck is he thinking? That's going to make my area hot." Marcheline huffed out a breath.

"We were thinking the same thing. If one of us has police up our asses, then it makes it bad for everybody."

With one eyebrow hiked high, he scrubbed his hand over his face. "Allen, was he a part of the side business?" Marcheline quizzed.

"He's dead, so we can't really talk to him at the moment," I answered.

Giosuè's mouth became a stern line spread across his

face. "The media hanging around those women and children will taint our legit businesses if it comes out that we had any business with Graziano."

An alert popped up on my phone that Giselle's sister had left work. I sent a text to Lake to keep an eye on her just in case she tried to contact Giselle.

"Giosuè, what are you proposing?" Marcheline wondered.

"For now, lock them down at your houses. I will personally give you triple the product to make up for the loss for the next two months," I interrupted their conversation.

"Are you equipped to cover that amount?" Marcheline quizzed.

"My cousin is carrying a large load of guns and drugs coming from Chicago. I personally vouch for him." Savio smirked and clapped me on the shoulder.

I stood and extended my hand.

"Savio, nice to see you again." Marcheline motioned at him.

"Marcheline, you all know me. If any of this stains my business, then you know I would be ready to completely remove every last one of you. I let my cousin take an extra piece of the pie."

"Six months," Geff spoke.

"We have the coverage of the women being taken away and getting care. Our lawyer is handling any blowback. The deal I am offering is a courtesy because it did touch you all in some way," Savio announced.

Geff held his hand up to whisper in Marcheline's ear, "Two shootouts are not a small issue."

"They wouldn't make a deal without being smart enough to call me first. I would have liked to know about a meeting if it pertained to my family," Titus hissed with a hard stare and a black cane appeared before Titus made a step toward the table.

Titus eased the chair back and sat down, glaring at everyone.

"Geff, prove us right and take the offer," Savio said.

"Fine," Geff responded.

I stood from my chair. "Before we agree, you have to tell us if you come in contact with Steele."

"We don't snitch Bosco." Marcheline shook his head.

I chuckled. "Either Steele, or your product comes up short."

All five of them glanced at each other and then peered at me.

"You have a deal."

Chapter Thirteen

Giselle

I turned off the ringing phone, exited my email, lifted my purse, strolled to my editor's office, knocked on the door, and pushed it open, not waiting for her to say anything. She hoisted her finger in the air, telling me to hold on, as she was on the phone. I stood near the entrance.

Andrea's teeth peeked through her lips. "Hey, sorry about that. You heading to lunch?"

"Yes, I wanted to let you know the article for Rose Thorn is sent to you."

Andrea typed on her computer. "Oh great, and the photos from the fashion show?"

"Being edited right now. Soon as I finish lunch, I will be back to look it over one more time."

"Great, thanks Giselle."

I hesitated before I walked off and smiled.

She squinted. "Is something wrong?"

"Do you have any siblings?" My heart burned with anxiety.

"I have an older brother." She sat back in her chair, crossing her legs.

"Would something make you turn your back on your family?"

Our conversation made her sit up, concerned. "I mean murder, but probably not." She tittered.

Our family fighting was rare—and no matter what, Mallory was my sister. "I better get going." I laughed.

"Are you sure you're all right?"

"I will be fine, really just need some food."

"If you need someone to talk to. I mean you saw your husband killed in front of you."

"Thanks, maybe you're right."

I sauntered out of the building and waved at Keith as he walked alongside me over to the cafe to meet my sister. She'd called me earlier, and at first, I was hesitant, but I decided to hear her out. I looked at some old pictures and text messages, but nothing stood out that signified she would be interested in having an affair with my husband.

I made it right on time and met her at the front entrance. She leaned forward to hug me, and I froze at her touch.

"Before we were fine and now it's like you've become someone else. What did I do?"

I placed my bag and phone down and removed my coat. "Be honest with me, Mallory."

There was never a time when my older sister was an enemy. Did I miss the signs?

She reached to cup my hand. "Always."

"Were you having an affair with Jason?"

Mallory spat out her drink.

"An affair!" she shrieked loudly.

I picked up her napkin to clean the spill on the top. "Shush, we are in public." I dropped my head in my hands.

Mallory held both her palms open. "Is that what has

you pissed off at me? Give me both of your hands, Gigi. I have never slept with that man."

"Nothing was going on with you two?" My voice cracked.

"Hell no! I thought he was cool, but Gigi, you're my baby sister. I would never hurt you that way. Now, that Bosco asshole can die a slow death." Mallory barked out a humorless laugh.

A giggle left my voice at her annoyance with Bosco, the two of them had clashed since day one. I understand her resistance because of how we got together.

The urge to call him and see what he was doing seeped through my mind. I gazed out the window, trying to find something or someone that looked familiar.

Mallory snapped her fingers in front of my face, knocking me from my daze. "Gigi!" She showed no signs of relenting on the Bosco situation.

"Yeah." I was certain now that I had deep feelings for him.

"Where did you go?"

I shook my head clear of the thoughts. "Uhm, nowhere." I fought hard not to laugh at her.

"You sure?" Determined to butt into my business, she held her cup in the air and motioned for another drink without getting up to order.

I smiled, picked up the glass of water, and gulped it down, convinced I must have been short on sleep to be seeing things.

"Anyway, Jason is not my type, and I have never wanted your husband. Besides, we barely spoke—unless you were around us."

"I believe someone was lying."

She smacked her lips. "Let me guess, Bosco."

I leaned back in chair, cocked my arm on the top corner. "No."

"Who then?"

"How are the kids?" I changed the subject.

"They miss you." Mallory's comfort zone was the pride and joy pertaining to her kids. They brought a softness that I liked to see.

I picked off a corner of her muffin and tossed it in my mouth.

"So, what do you think about going shopping to catch up?"

I lifted my wrist to check the time. "Rain check. I can go after work. I have to approve pictures for the fashion event for my editor."

"I heard you kicked ass with the article." A relieved look washed over her face.

"Mom must have called you." I laughed.

Her shoulders softly sagged. Mallory finished her drink. "She's wondering when you're going to call her."

"I will do it tonight."

"Glad you've come to your senses."

I reached over and grabbed a fry off her plate. "Bosco is my boyfriend, Mallory; it won't change."

Mallory rolled her eyes and smacked my hand away. "Tell me you're in love without telling me you're in love."

"Stop being mean, and we're not at the *love* stage yet." Sometimes I preferred to keep my personal relationships away from my sister.

"Lie to your parents, but not your sister." My sister had the idea that one day I'd grow up and follow her exact life choices, but it never happened.

"Give him a chance, I think you might find him to be sweet."

"Sour in my book," Mallory mumbled, with an identical remake of our mother's face.

We cackled at her comment and finished our meal.

Two hours later I came back to the office and confirmed the photos for the article, when that flash of a figure coming out of the bank earlier popped in my head.

"I closed our joint accounts after Jason died," I muttered, logged into my old email account, and scanned through statements.

Chase Bank sent their last communication a year ago, which was weird because I closed the account *four* years ago. I hadn't looked into my personal email for years since work took up much of my time, and I moved all my money to an individual account. A sharp pang stung my chest at the withdrawal of money that had happened every six weeks.

"Hey, Giselle."

I clicked away from my email account and smiled at Colleen. "Hi."

"Congrats again on your billboard." Her hair framed her face; it was silvery blonde, and she wore it straight and long.

"Billboard?"

The sheer logic of me and billboard made no sense.

"Yes, you can't miss it or have you been sleeping off today?" Colleen laughed.

"Sorry, Colleen, I have no clue what you're talking about."

Colleen walked to her cubicle and stretched her hand for her phone, typed on it, and held it up to my face. "Here, I took video and a picture."

On the screen, I saw a huge billboard with my face and

the name of my magazine, including the article on Rose Thorn.

My eyes raised to Colleen, then went back down to the phone in confusion. "Where—I mean, who?" My career was the most important thing to me. It had become natural to work hard and never be seen. Other people paid large sums of money to get their work noticed.

"Seriously you didn't know?"

I jumped up from my desk and snatched her phone out of her hand. "I have a billboard. Colleen my face is on a billboard in Times Square."

Colleen cheesed. "Isn't it exciting? The bigwigs are praising you, and I heard you might be doing 'Good Morning, America.'"

"*Jesus.*"

"Someone that has a lot of money and power has your back because it is hard to do."

I snapped my fingers. "Money...Bosco."

"Who?"

I gave Colleen her phone and grabbed my things to leave for the day. "My boy—Nothing. I have to go."

I ransacked my purse as I waited for the elevator to come up to my floor. I lifted my ringing phone and saw Bosco's name—just the one person I wanted to talk to about the billboard. After another person jumped on as I moved around them, I answered and heard loud wind in the background.

"Gigi."

"Hi." Hope was one thing I was deprived of for a long time, but Bosco had opened my mind to so many possibilities.

"Hearing your voice makes me smile." Even just hearing his voice while we were apart made me feel desirable.

"Glad I could make your day."

"Same, how is work going?"

Love was a weed that flourished in the dark, since Bosco I knew I could have happiness without the trauma. "Work is fine, actually leaving right now."

"You had lunch with your sister, correct?"

I sighed and cleared my throat. "Yes, and Mallory explained they never had an affair."

"You believe her."

The very thought of the situation put a damper on my excitement from Colleen, but I wouldn't let it consume me.

"Yes, Allen would try and throw anyone under the bus to save himself."

"Allen would lie, but Mallory hates that you're dating me."

I would give him a proper thank you in the bedroom when we were alone, for now a quick one had to happen.

"Mallory's not the topic right now. I wanted to say thank you."

"Thank you for what?" A hint of a smile appeared in his voice.

"Colleen informed me a life size picture of me and my article on Rose Thorn is plastered on a billboard in Times Square."

"Is it now, I wonder who would go to such lengths?" He was not a man that liked attention.

"Mhmmm, a guy with a smooth voice, around 6'1"-6'2", sexy lips, a smile that makes my panties wet."

"Stop teasing me, Gigi," Bosco growled.

"Now why would I tease you Bosco?" I purred, peering around to make sure all eyes weren't on me.

"Where are you?"

"Heading home."

"Damn, I wish I could meet you, but I have a few things I need to clean up."

"Something that can wait?" I was used to him moving quickly to make me feel prioritized.

"Bosco! They're ready," I heard someone yell in the background.

"I got to go *Una donna splendida*," Bosco said.

I never got tired of him calling me gorgeous in Italian.

Our nights lately had ended with me in his arms, and the protection of his kisses showed he cared and let the hard exterior go only for me.

"Hurry home, I'm going to call the girls to do some shopping and then we can do dinner together. I want to say thank you in person."

"I can't wait." Bosco dropped the call.

The sun caressed my cheek as my eyes roamed through the streets of New York. Mikell stopped at a light while I sent a text to Rena.

Me: *Ladies, can you believe what Bosco did as a surprise?*

Rena: *Giselle! That is Times Square. Oh, my God.*

Mckayla: *I can barely get Savio to let me out of the house*

and your man is buying billboards.

I chuckled at Mckayla's response, and my gaze stopped at the Chase bank I saw earlier when I had lunch with my sister.

Rena: *Hell, even Renato flies Penelope to wine country once a month.*

Me: *Sorry ladies, but Bosco has topped them all.*

"Mikell, can you pull over at the bank please?"

"The bank?"

I pointed at Chase bank on the right of the road.

"Yes ma'am," Mikell replied, and he adjusted the mirror in the window.

Keith came around to hold the door. I held my hand up to stop him and stared through the lobby. I pulled up my old email address on my phone and waited in line as Keith stepped to the side and monitored the area. The sunlight hit each corner of the room; they'd upgraded some of the chairs and opened more space for cashiers.

"Hello, welcome to Chase bank."

"Hi, I wanted to ask about an old account I closed."

"Sure, can you give me the name?"

"Jason Ford."

"Do you have ID?" the bank teller questioned.

I handed over my license and waited as she typed on the computer. "It's a joint account with me and my husband. Jason and Giselle Ford."

"Seems like the account wasn't closed, ma'am."

I hoisted the pen to write out the dates. "That can't be correct; I came in here myself three years ago."

She looked back at the computer, then back at me. "Sorry Mrs. Ford, the account was never closed."

I dropped the pen on the counter. "What is the last transaction?"

"Actually, today, a withdrawal of $100,000."

I thumbed the top of the counter, nibbled on my top lip. "Thank you."

She started to close the window. "No problem, thank you for banking with Chase."

"Wait! Can you tell me who took out the money?"

"It shows the money was done with our banker since the amount was high."

"Thanks."

I walked away, and Keith trekked in front of me, holding

the entrance door. I got back in the car and checked the time on my phone.

* * *

The crowds weren't heavy, which meant our outing didn't need much security. Rena held her shopping bags, sipping on her iced latte as we marched into Chanel.

"The bank teller said the account is still open," Mckayla said and handed Rena a purse.

"Maybe get that clutch in red," Rena remarked and handed me a belt to look at.

The click of heels moved around us, a few more shoppers popped inside.

"Strange, I personally walked in the bank and closed the account."

Rena gulped on her drink. "I mean maybe you forgot and had someone close it for you."

"No, I mean my mom helped me organize the funeral, and Mallory took care of the catering, but the important papers and Jason's things I packed up for his family."

Mckayla picked up another clutch bag and held it up to the light. "His father has given you problems in the past."

"Corbin didn't have access to our accounts."

Rena gathered two purses and handed them to the Chanel associate. "Are you sure? I mean, you said his entire family was overbearing when you got married."

Mckayla sipped on the champagne that was offered to buyers. "Ohh, I like the black-and-white dress." Mckayla spun to face us.

"Bosco and my sister don't get along, my ex-father-in-law tried to have me sold into sex trafficking, and my father has worked undercover with the mob for a few years. I think I deserve more than one Chanel bag," I joked.

Rena and Mckayla's eyes connected at my rant.

The hostess brought another tray of drinks, but Mckayla waved her away. "Maybe something stronger will help you."

"I need to dig into it more."

Rena brandished a belt in front of us. "What if you find something that you shouldn't?"

I shrugged and wagged my finger to get a different style. "Jason already made my life hard when he stole from Bosco's family."

A worry line formed on Mckayla's forehead. "Just be careful."

Rena stretched her legs in front of her and took a seat. "I'll help."

"Aren't you and Sante flying back to Chicago?"

"Nope, I told him we should stay a little longer, he wants to find this Steele guy."

"Sante tells you everything when it comes to his business."

"He has no choice; I like to snoop around his office too much." Rena snickered and passed over her credit card to pay for her items.

The girls kept me laughing while we shopped, then we had Keith take them back to the hotel they were staying in with their husbands. We made it back home before seven. Keith grabbed my shopping bags. I tucked my purse under my arm, unlocked the house, let him walk through first, and left my bags on the floor near the banister.

"Thank you, Keith."

"Yes, ma'am."

"Hello, Miss Giselle." Yun appeared at the ledge of the stairs.

I stopped and turned to head into the kitchen. "Hi, Yun." I popped the fridge open. "Is dinner ready?"

Yun moved to the entryway and picked up my bags. "It is—and Mr. Bosco is waiting for you. I can bring these up for you."

"Great. Thank you, Yun." I grabbed a bottled water out of the fridge and searched for Bosco in his office, then the theater room.

"Bosco!" I called from the hallway.

"In the bedroom."

I climbed upstairs, ready to talk about our day. "Dinner's ready."

"Come here."

"Dinner's going to get cold," I said, ambling upstairs to the bedroom. I opened the door and gasped in delight.

The entire room was dark, with candles lit up along a trail, and soft music was playing. A pleasant smell lingered in the air. My heart leaped for joy as words clogged my voice at what he'd done for me. I'd already had plans to surprise him, but he'd once again left me speechless.

Chapter Fourteen

Bosco

My gaze took hold of her, like a perfect ballerina she moved with grace and elegance.

"You didn't have to do this, Bosco." Her hair hung off her shoulder.

I extended my hand to guide her through the pathway to the dinner table. "Come closer."

Gigi held her hand on her heart, pressed her lips together, and smiled. "Dinner on the balcony."

Even before she called, I had plans to do something special for us without any disturbance from the family.

I eased the chair for her to sit. "I know we've had a lot of craziness happening. I wanted you to relax tonight, eat, watch a movie, then maybe a massage."

Gigi drew closer and smelled the roses on the table. They grew in abundance in the garden, and I had Yun pick a few to top off the special occasion.

"Dinner sounds lovely, and it smells good. Yun cooked everything."

"She talked to your mom and got your favorites, and I brought the wine."

Gigi was lavishly attractive; she could make a man fall to his knees and give her anything she wanted without question. "Somehow, you knew I would need a night like this."

"Busy at work?"

"Yes, and you know I had lunch with Mallory, plus shopping with the girls."

I interlocked our hands and held my glass of Moet with the other. "Sante got the text messages of the purchases Rena made and he's already trying to keep you two apart."

"Rena's the best."

"Penelope wants to hang with you guys, since work has calmed down for her."

"Is Giosuè okay with us hanging out together?"

The tip of my tongue traced my lips. "He has no choice. If he had a problem with it, then Penelope would start ignoring him, like I do whenever he tries to act like the boss." I laid my napkin on my lap, poured Gigi some white wine, and filled my glass too.

"A toast."

My pretty lady offered one of those mesmerizing looks. "To you and the way you make me smile."

Without her even having to touch me, my dick throbbed ready to be inside of her. "A smile is good, but I like the moans better."

Goosebumps clothed her wrist and arm. "I bet you do." Gigi licked her lips, tapping her hand on the top of the table. "Can I tell you something, and you won't freak out?"

I cleaned my mouth and nodded. "Go ahead."

"It might not be anything, but I thought I saw Jason today."

"Where?"

"I was at lunch with Mallory, and I happened to look out the window, and it looked like he was outside the bank."

Fear engulfed her mood, and I hated the hold he still had on her life.

A sense of peace is what I wanted for her to know.

"He's dead." I chugged my drink. In my line of business, we saw it all, and families often fantasized about the people they lost still roaming the earth. Seeing her caught in a web of lies really burned me; she would have been better off if Jason divorced her.

"You could be right, but I checked my old email and saw I had a few statements from my old bank account."

"Did you see anything else weird?"

She tucked a long loose strand behind her ear. "That's the thing. I closed the account three years ago, but a year ago they started back up again with transactions."

"What are you saying?" Concern grew on my face as I listened.

"Nothing. I think maybe long hours and stress from everything has caught up to me."

The idea of leaving the craziness behind sparked an idea in my brain to take her away and let my brothers handle things. "We should go on a trip."

"A trip...so good." A soft moan escaped her lips from the baked lobster mac and cheese.

Lobster sauce dripped from my fork as I dragged it to my lips. "A trip just the two of us together, soon as you can get free from work."

"Then I can wear my new clothes I got from Chanel."

I slipped my hand into my pocket, removed my wallet, and handed her my American Express card. "Which reminds me—you should be using my credit card."

"What's this?"

Our women never paid for a thing. It was futile to disagree, and I forced it toward her. "Credit card."

Gigi finished the last little bit of food on her plate. A little fell on her cheek, and she raised her napkin to clean her face. "I get that, but why are you giving it to me?"

"My money is yours."

Gigi turned away and patted tears from her eyes. "Bosco, you're kidding."

"No, and I transferred $20,000 back into your account from today's shopping trip."

"I like you for you, not the money."

I saw myself as a bull, and the world was my grassland, but Gigi saw something different, and I wanted her to never get used to the bull—unless it was to save her life. "Same."

"Bosco! I'm serious, you are more than what I expected."

"I expect you to use that card going forward."

"And my baby Prince?" she jested and fluttered her lashes playfully.

I had to play it safe, so I wouldn't end up celibate like a monk. My cousins had animals, but our parents never allowed them in our home.

"The little—"

"Be nice." She giggled. Her breasts spilled from her shirt when she leaned on the table.

"Spoil your little doggy."

She sent a wink in my direction as she slowly rose from her chair. "Well, I guess I need to repay you somehow."

The night we slept together replayed in my mind. Gigi became mine, and each time I devoured her sweet skin, it sent a shock to my system. It felt like my brain and heart wanted to protect her from those who would put her in danger at all times, because the second she touched me, Hell would not even be the safest place for them to hide. I gazed at her and drew in a deep breath. My mouth watered at her slowly bending down onto her knees in front of me as the sun went down. Without asking for help, she unzipped my pants, tucked her hand in, and removed my dick. *Prince can stay forever.* Her head bobbed up and down. She moaned and popped it out of her mouth. Over and over, she did the exact same move, and I hit the back of her throat again and again.

"Giselle, stop playing with me," I growled.

My pretty lady hummed through a moan. I slid a hand across her back, down to her ass, and smacked both cheeks and caressed up and down.

"Fuck me on the bed," Giselle said.

"No, I have a better idea."

I pulled my pants up, helped her up, walked out of bedroom and down to the garage, then slid the door closed.

Giselle stood with her hand on her hip. "What are you up to, Bosco?"

"Come here." I tossed my jacket on top of the hood of my car, snatched Giselle to my chest, and removed my dick through my briefs. I helped Giselle to climb on my bike, slid her panties to the side, and pulled her on top of my dick.

"Baby, hold on!"

I turned the key, revved the bike, and slowly pumped in. I watched her mouth open and close. An intense level of noise blocked out any sounds of her moans throughout the house and kept my soldiers away. I often repaired my bike in the garage and did work to keep my mind busy. Yun would often find me hiding away in the garage for hours, sometimes without eating, and she would have to leave my food in the oven.

The force of my pumps with her legs locked around my waist—the position gave her no relief. A mutual shudder ran across us both.

"Ughh, fuck." A gentle, passionate moan escaped her lips.

"You wanted to be fucked, take this dick like a good little bitch," I snarled in her ear.

Anytime I could see her under my spell, at my fingertip of lust, filled my hunger and gave me satisfaction.

Right as I circled my hips, I leaned forward, kissed her on the cheek, opened the door with my remote, and slowly rolled into the driveway. Giselle's eyes popped open, and she tried to sit up.

"Don't move," I growled.

"Bosco!" Her fingers fumbled to hold on.

I smirked. "You're afraid, but your pussy is getting wetter and wetter baby."

Her hands grasped my arms. I moved back inside the garage, parked, and turned the bike off. Giselle rocked on top of me, surging with physical excitement. I wrapped both hands around her waist and sucked on her breasts.

I held onto her and moved her up against the wall, then turned her around, eased back inside, and pushed her hands above her head. My stomach twisted with a hard knot of need as slow warmth spread through her limbs as she covered my dick.

The rhythm of licking and sucking on her neck, I spread her ass apart and moved the head of my dick to her asshole, and she froze.

I kissed her forehead, cheek, and lips. "Relax. Just breathe for me."

"Umm...ooh, so good."

The sound of sex was the only reality in the garage. I glided my dick into her tight asshole inch by inch. Feeling Giselle shaking, I kissed along her shoulder.

"Gigi, I will kill you if you ever take this away from me." I groaned, then released prematurely.

"Fuck!"

Giselle giggled, turned around, slung her arms around my shoulders, and plunged her body close to mine. "Someone's a quick pumper."

I slapped her on the ass. "I'll take a rain check, the pussy is too good."

We both cackled at my joke, fixed ourselves up enough to head back into the house, went to the bathroom, turned on the shower, and turned it up to steaming hot. Gigi stepped in front of me and grabbed the body wash and towel, then washed my back. I tossed my head back and felt her soft hands move around me in circular motions. She nudged me under the faucet to clean me off. She pressed kisses along my chest, stood on her tiptoes, and sucked on my neck.

I cupped her ass, spread it apart, and played with her pussy.

"Ahhhh... oohh, yes."

I lifted her up and plunged into her pussy, rough and raw lovemaking.

"That's right. Feel all of me, baby."

Her breasts jiggled in front of my face, I removed one hand from her ass, cupped her left breast, and sucked on her nipple.

"Fuck, Bosco... keep it there." She panted; her eyes rolled into the back of her head.

I turned us around with her back against the wall and pumped faster and faster.

The sounds of our skin slapping together filled the bathroom. Most of the house heard her screams, and I hated that they had the pleasure of knowing what she sounded like, but I couldn't stop myself from thrusting harder and harder.

"All you needed, baby girl." My thrusts were slow and steady.

She nodded and passionately arched her back to meet me.

"Let me hear you." The fires of expectation were out of control.

"Yes, I'm coming!" she screamed and fell onto my chest as she came.

I stared at her pussy contracting around my dick, the moment of ecstasy exploded in my chest.

* * *

The thought of seeing Jason at the bank still came to mind as Gigi fell asleep in my arms. I shot him from a distance, and had my team clean it up, but I never stayed the entire time and now, I wondered if he was buried for real.

Would Gigi lie to me?

While the house was quiet, I puffed on a cigar and scanned through the news articles from the day of his shooting. Each one showed that he was buried at Memorial Lincoln Cemetery. There were pictures of Gigi, her family, and Jason's family surrounding the casket. I dialed Armani's number from the landline and waited for him to pick up. It was going on ten at night, and he was usually at the club, unless he was working on collections.

"You should be here at work," Armani expressed.

"Could someone on your team not finish the job?" There was nothing worse than incompetence—or flat-out betrayal.

"What are you asking?"

"The clean-up crew you vetted."

"People I hand selected." Armani grimaced.

I sat forward, leaning my elbows on the desk. "Gigi thought she saw her ex today."

"Her dead husband?"

I brushed my hand down my face. "Sounds crazy, but what if she's right?" I felt a stab of regret.

"She could be stressed from what happened with Steele." Armani was rich, single, smart, and more of a leader than either me or Giosuè would ever be. I ragged on him a lot, but his craziness could only be contained for so long until someone tried to push his buttons. People would think that getting advice from a younger sibling was strange, but as the enforcer, he had more insight after going to school for psychology.

The chair squeaked as I slumped down and stretched out my legs. "Could be, I think a lot is happening, and Allen's shit was a lie about her sister."

"I'm leaving the club; I can come by there, or you can meet me."

"Gigi's asleep, I can't sneak out right now."

"Meet in the morning."

I grabbed the mouse, clicked to another camera screen, and stared at my sleeping beauty. "I want to start with the cemetery first thing in the morning." The image melted away the dark cloud of bullshit around me.

"Giosuè will be pissed if this is true."

I furrowed my brows at Prince sleeping at the foot of my bed. "He's not the only one, some people are going to die."

"I agree, let me wrap up here."

"Armani?"

"I'm here."

"You want a dog?" Somehow, Prince knew I was talking

about him, because he happened to wake up and stare up at the bed.

"No, and he's harmless."

I grunted. "Harmless my ass. Anyway, Jason's going to wish he were dead."

"That's the Bosco I know, and call your sister sometimes."

I bobbed my head, peering at a photo of us all together in Italy when I was younger. "I will." I ended the call, placed the phone back on the receiver, shut down the computer, turned the light out, curled up under the sheets, pulled Gigi close in my arms, and kissed her shoulder.

* * *

The following day, before Gigi could question me, I met up with my soldiers to research what she'd found out at the bank. I removed my black shades and stared at Paul, one of the directors at the cemetery that we'd used a few times to bury some people without the police finding the body.

"Mr. Calabresi, how can I help you today?"

Armani rode with me to Lincoln Cemetery, he'd already flipped the sign to *closed* so we were not disturbed.

I chewed down my kill first and ask questions last mind frame and smiled. "Paul, I need your help in locating a boy."

Paul pulled up his database. "Okay, who?"

"Jason Ford."

He typed on his computer, then stared at me. "A Jason Ford was buried four years ago."

"We know, I need to see the actual body."

Paul's brow pulled together in confusion. "Are you talking about digging up a body?'

"Yes."

His eyes darted between me and Armani. "Mr. Calabresi, I know we've done a few things for you in the past, but this would be going against a few laws."

I laid my hand on top of the computer and twisted it to face me. "You make how much money here, Paul?"

"Mr. Calabresi, it's not about the money." He took stock of the change in my tone.

"Then your life."

He gulped down the threat. "I have a reputation. Families want to make sure that their loved ones are taken care of here," Paul insisted, staring from me to Armani, and then to my other soldiers in the office.

I snatched a peppermint from the candy dish and tossed it in my mouth. "Paul, we know your family would hate to have to deal with burying you on top of finding a new business after we burn Memorial Cemetery down."

Paul grabbed his keys, walked to the door, locked it behind him, walked through the back employee entrance, and led us to the grounds where the burial plots were. Across the large trees, we made it to Jason Ford's grave, and I bent down and read the plaque that stated *Jason Ford, Loving Husband and Son.*

I gestured to my crew. "Dig it up."

Paul jumped in front of me with his hands up in the air. "Wait a minute, you can't be serious, Mr. Calabresi that's highly irresponsible and immoral."

Armani's grin was lopsided, like two sides of a trick coin. "Immoral only to *you.*"

I grabbed Paul by both shoulders and moved him to the side. "Paul if you don't want to join him, you better stay back."

Armani and I talked amongst ourselves as we watched

them dig. A few hours turned to late afternoon when they made it to the casket.

"Boss, we might have a problem!" Charley, one of my crew members, exclaimed, wiping his forehead.

I moved in closer and glanced at the empty casket that should have had a body inside that I personally killed.

"Where's the body?" Paul inquired, and blotches of red erupted on his cheeks.

I eased my hand on the holster and removed the gun. "Good question, Paul, and you better get to talking."

Paul took a step back as Armani and I moved in closer to him. Suddenly, he dropped to the ground, and gunshots passed by us in the cemetery.

"Fuck, get down."

Ratta Rattta!

I leaped behind a tree, scanned the streets, and saw a car speed away before I could aim back at them.

Armani pulled out his cell. "We need to call Giosuè."

I leaned my head against the tree, cursed, and closed my eyes, aggravated at being caught out in the open with less security detail.

"I will get the clean-up crew to the cabin and find out what we missed. Maybe Steele paid them off?" Armani wondered.

"Keep me posted, I will talk to Giosuè, headed to him now."

"What about Paul?"

I pointed at the casket where Jason's body was supposed to be buried. "Bury him. Have a free casket right there."

* * *

Four Years Ago

I tossed the cigarette to the ground, finished reading the text from Armani, started the engine, as sirens blared in the air.

Our leader on the clean-up crew talked to someone on the phone, and he glanced over. We made eye contact as I saluted in acknowledgement at seeing Jason's body wrapped up in a black bag.

*

Chapter Fifteen

Giselle

All I could think about was a weekend on the road with my hair down, laughter in the air, great food, and alcoholic drinks, along with kisses from my boyfriend. Instead, I was there at my old apartment, going through old paperwork that I'd boxed up and couldn't take the time to look through when Jason died. Bosco was still asleep in bed after working late again, but he promised we could do something when he fully got some rest. I was not sure what happened, but he was on edge and stressed. I sat on my bedroom floor with piles of boxes scattered around, along with wedding photos, books, love letters, and old bills that Jason and I had together.

Mallory carried in another box and set it on the ground. After she had breakfast with her family, she'd come to meet me. "Is there something specific you're looking for, Gigi?"

She drifted to the vanity mirror and picked up a bottle of perfume, then sprayed it in the air to smell it.

"No, just wondering when I closed the joint account."

Mallory put the perfume back, ambled in my direction,

and plopped down beside me. "I see some old tax returns here, and a few bank statements."

"Pass them here."

I flipped through the folder, and everything seemed like typical bank logs and transactions. I paused and stared up at the ceiling.

"I think we should break and go have lunch with Mom."

As I nodded in agreement, I read over each document rapidly. "Okay, maybe you're right. I mean, the account could be an error."

My sister extended her hand with the phone for me to take. "Call the bank and close it again."

"True, I could have the money transferred to a charity or something."

She cast a glower back at me. "Charity? That's your money. Why not keep it for yourself?"

I bumped her shoulder and stood. "Mallory, it's blood money."

"To who? Your boyfriend's a gangster. I think you are past having standards."

That last part had me rolling my eyes. I tossed the papers back on the bed. "Please, not today. Come on, call Mom, and see what she's cooking."

Mallory dialed Mom on her phone, holding up a picture. "Giselle, take a look at this picture. I've never seen him before."

I paused as I opened the front door, turned to face Mallory, gazed at the picture, and greeted Keith. We stepped outside to leave. I froze and stared at a photo of Corbin, Jason, and the man that took me hostage. The empty soulless eyes stared back, I covered my face with a hand in shock that Corbin and Jason knew someone that dealt with human trafficking.

Mallory snapped her fingers at me, breaking me out of my dazed state. "Are you all right, Giselle? Do you know him?"

"Uhm, no. Let's go. I know Mom cooked a lot of food."

"If something is wrong, you can talk to me."

Ring

"I have to take this call."

A loud motorcycle roar blared in front of my stoop. I smiled, declined the call, approached Bosco, and waited for him to remove his helmet. It felt like a daydream when I saw him appear, like he knew I needed his presence without me asking. "You finally woke up." I stole a kiss, brushing a hand up his arm.

Bosco passed the helmet to me. "Hop on. Let's go for a ride."

I poked my top lip out and stomped my foot. "Mallory has plans for us to have lunch with my mom."

He looked over my shoulder. "Can you reschedule, I want to take you on a date."

"A date?" I grinned and swallowed the urge to squeal in his ear in excitement.

My sister crept up and mushed me on the arm. "Giselle, we have plans."

"Mallory," Bosco said, dryly like it would hurt to say hello.

"Asshole," Mallory grumbled; her body was rigid with tension.

"You two have to get along." My words fell dead and brittle like oak leaves in fall. "I want you both in my life, so agree to disagree, but you need to be nice in front of me."

A sigh caught in her throat. "That's going to be hard." As the oldest, I expected more from Mallory.

"I have no problems with your sister."

"You accused me of sleeping with her husband." The words tore from her throat.

I studied his face, then turned to her. "That wasn't coming from Bosco."

She sucked her teeth. "He probably paid the guy off to turn you against me."

"Mallory..." I pleaded, brushing my hand on her arm.

"I have lunch planned for us and then you can hang with your family. I have something to finish anyway that will take up time."

"Mallory, do you mind if I take a rain check on lunch?"

"Tell that to Mommy."

Bosco thrust out a hand and kissed my palm. "How about we invite your family to my house for dinner, we can have a do-over from last time."

I climbed on the back of the bike and pressed a kiss to his neck. "Actually, that would be great." My family and Bosco had to get along for us to move forward as a long-term couple. I realized that during our last intimate moments we never used a condom. Even with Jason, I planned to have kids, but it never happened.

"Mallory come on, please be nice and I will call Mom."

Bosco pushed the engine of the bike and moved to turn into traffic, the sun beamed down on my skin. Mallory walked over to her car and smiled back at me.

"Where are we going anyway?"

"To have lunch, then I have a friend you might like to meet."

"Who is your friend?" I sat forward to kiss him on the lips. "Is this friend a woman you dated?"

Bosco chuckled and approached the middle of traffic. He slowed down at the stop sign, turned left, and headed in the direction of Brooklyn.

I laid my head on his back and felt the wind in my hair, along with the calmness and protection that came with being near him. Bosco's attention shocked me, but the way he counted on his brothers, his cousins, and their wives showed that he protected the people he loved.

My daydreaming paused when we arrived at the Brooklyn Botanical Garden.

Bosco helped me down, and I clasped his hand and walked into an empty room. "Usually, it's crazy busy in here."

He buried his face in my neck, left me with goosebumps of pleasure. "I rented it out for today."

I froze in surprise. "The entire Garden?"

Sneakily, Bosco snuggled close, slipped his tongue into my mouth, and pecked me on the lips. "I know you love flowers; I wanted to have a chance to make it right after the flowers I sent to your place when I first met you."

"Bosco, you make me speechless."

"Come on, I want to take advantage while we can. We only have the place for two hours."

One of the workers gave us a tour and pointed toward our table for lunch.

"It's beautiful here."

"I thought you'd like something simple; I know my money doesn't make you excited like some women."

"A guy that tries to impress me with his money could never get my attention, but I don't want to go down that road, I have something to tell you."

The staff had roasted mushroom soup, seared cod basquaise, along with Chardonnay.

"Go ahead."

"When I went to my old apartment, I searched for the bank stuff I told you about."

"I told you to let me handle it, Gigi."

"I get it, and we didn't really find anything at first."

Bosco's right brow raised at my statement.

I reached into my pocket and placed the picture on the top of the table. I raised the wine and swirled it in my hand before gulping it down.

He loomed forward with clasped hands. "A picture?"

"Look at it and tell me what I'm seeing is not a dream."

Bosco grabbed the picture, and his face went from curious to angry in the blink of an eye. "Where did you find this picture?" An array of secrets might come from what I had discovered.

"Mallory found it in one of my boxes of papers I had packed away."

His gaze took hold, searing into the abyss at an alarming rate. "Corbin, Jason, and Spook."

"Spook?"

"The third man who held you hostage, one of Steele's minions." Silence lingered in the moment; steam would have come out of my ears if this were a cartoon.

I shoved more soup in my mouth.

"He's dead now, can't hurt you."

"When will all this be over? Corbin hasn't contacted me since the fashion show." My voice cracked against the quiet air.

"He's not stupid to come out again and show his face."

"Jason really turned my life into a shit show." Greed was the real reason he was blinded.

Our fingers interlocked while we continued to eat. Bosco tipped my chin up. "Hey, don't cry. I'm here, and I won't let him or anyone else hurt you."

"I feel safe with you Bosco, but who is keeping you safe?"

He grinned. "Never worry about me, *amora*."

Nobody could snatch that smile from his lips. I enjoyed seeing the calm, relaxed, and fun side of him. My next goal was to get him on board with becoming friends with Prince.

* * *

After Bosco treated me to a wonderful date, I felt like it would be a great compromise to get both our worlds together.

I held a large salad bowl and laid it in the middle of the table, then greeted Mom and Dad when they appeared in the living room.

Dad walked up to me and kissed me on the forehead, Mom hugged me tight and peered around the dining table at the other guests at the table.

"I thought it was just the family," Mallory said.

A few voices broke through the threshold and crossed into the dining room. I gestured for them to come closer to introduce them. "My family and Bosco's family are here in town, so I thought it would be nice to see everybody."

The men stood alongside their wives.

Rena stuck her hand up in the air. "Hi, I'm Rena, Sante's wife and friends with your daughter."

"Mallory, her older sister," my sister said.

Rena's eyes clouded with disapproval. "The one that slept with the old husband."

Silence lingered in the air, along with Prince eating from his bowl.

"Rena!" Sante and I spoke at the same time.

Savio laughed at the outburst, and my parents looked embarrassed.

"I can clear that up right now. Jason and I never slept

together. I love my sister, and even though she wants to stay with *him*, I will respect her decision," Mallory exclaimed.

"Hi, ignore Rena. My name's Mckayla, married to Savio, the grouch."

Savio frowned. Mckayla kissed him on the cheek, and he smiled.

"Please take your seats, Rena be nice," I whispered in her ear.

Yun cooked a large spread. Bosco sat at the head of the table, and I eased next to him. My mom and dad sat beside me with Mallory on the end of the table. Savio, Sante, Rena, and Mckayla lifted their utensils and napkins to start eating.

"Mr. Calabresi, I wanted to apologize for our lack of manners when we first met you," Mom began to talk and watched the expression on Dad's face turn sour.

We talked on the phone a few times, but the shift in our relationship since living with Bosco had shown in their lack of coming around me. In the past Mom and I would have a weekly date night, then family dinners, and I barely even get a phone call now.

"Giselle, has told me about how much she's missed you all and I understand it can look odd from the outside, but I care for your daughter very much," Bosco announced.

"Aaron, how is retirement going?" Savio probed.

"Fine," Dad said through gritted teeth, then drank the rest of his beer.

Rena clapped her hands in excitement. "Giselle, did you tell your parents about your billboard picture?"

Mom looked from Rena to me. "Billboard?"

I lifted my phone, went to the photo, and showed her. "Bosco surprised me with the article I did for Rose Thorn and put it on a billboard in Times Square."

"Wow, a billboard in Times Square? I'm impressed."

Prince wagged his tail, lingering under my chair. I cupped his paw. "Thank you. Bosco also does little things, on top of the extravagant ones."

"Can I speak to you, Giselle, in the other room?" Dad asked.

"Uh, sure." I rose from the chair, bent down, kissed Bosco on the cheek, then followed my dad into the hallway.

He folded his arms and paced back and forth, the man I knew would sacrifice his life for his family, seemed different.

"Dad, are you all right?"

He shifted his feet. "No, have you spoken to Corbin lately?"

I leaned back on the wall and stared at him. "Corbin? Hold up. Why is Corbin calling you?"

"Calm down, it was a surprise to me as well."

"You two have never been close, so tell me." My heart was beating fast with apprehension.

Dad reached to stroke my cheek. "He asked me if I'd talked with you about visiting Jason's burial plot lately."

I stepped back out of his touch. "Burial plot?" I considered what this all meant.

"Yeah, I was confused, but he said there was a shootout and the owner was killed."

"Paul is dead?" Every nerve in my body seemed to shrink.

"I don't want to think it, but has Bosco mentioned anything about Jason at the cemetery?"

"No, I mean I told him about—" For a moment, I pondered whether I should avoid talking about my past so we could truly move forward.

Those strong arms wrapped around me before I even heard his voice. "Is something wrong, amora?"

My father half turned to face me. "No, I just wanted to clear some stuff up with my daughter."

I tugged on his arm. "Dad, wait."

He kissed me on the forehead and hugged me. "You be careful, Giselle. I don't know what is going on, but if I need to call up some of my buddies, I will."

Bosco turned me around to face him. "Talk to me."

I scratched the side of my arm. "Honestly, I have no clue what is going on—and it's probably nothing—but the owner of Lincoln Cemetery was really nice and helped me a lot when Jason died."

Bosco held me close to his chest, brushing his hand up and down my back. "Seems Jason's death has touched a lot of people's lives."

Bosco raised my chin and pecked me on the mouth. I smiled.

"We should go back and finish eating. I know Rena is probably trying to give my sister the evil eye."

He pinched my cheek, nudged me close, we whipped around, and headed back into the dining room for dinner.

Yun cleaned up the plates. Mom offered to help, and I forced her to relax and drink some wine with the rest of the girls. As night came, all the men were holed up in Bosco's office, and I hated that we had to split into groups, but Bosco had a call he needed to take.

Mom placed both hands on my shoulders, then gripped both of my hands. "Mallory and I talked with your dad. We're very proud of you, Gigi, and we want the best for you."

"Thanks, Mom."

"If Bosco is who you love, then we will support you."

"Pretty *lady*," Bosco said, affection in his voice.

She grinned, patted me on the back, and placed her

hand on the couch. "We see it all over your face. You can't hide it from your momma."

"He's an asshole, but I guess he got you a nice home." I loved when Mallory was being a jokester.

"I agree with you on that one." Rena laughed, raising her glass in the air to salute Mallory.

The two of them seemed to have let their walls down and were getting along so far.

I excused myself and went to find the men. I heard loud shouts from the other side of his office door.

"He's missing!" Dad shouted.

I turned the knob and burst through inside. "Who's missing?"

The guys stared at each other, then at me. I felt like something was wrong, and everybody knew except for me.

Dad walked up to me. "Honey."

"I will tell her." Bosco groaned.

There, just around the corners of each mind, men as usual butted heads trying to be the leader of a family. Their perception probably felt I should stay in my place, but I operated differently now.

"Fine, but if something happens to my daughter..." Hatred seeped from his mouth.

"Dad, tonight is about us mending fences. Bosco is there something I should know?"

Bosco shook his head. "Later." His demeanor went back into underboss mode.

Dad looked from me to Bosco and stomped out of the office, Savio and Sante stood, along with Armani, and gave me sympathetic looks.

"Come on let's go enjoy your family and worry about other stuff later."

"You promise to keep me in the loop?" Pain swayed through my mind.

He clasped an arm around my shoulder, leaned in, and smiled. "I promise."

Tonight's dinner was a little rocky, but we were able to coexist as a family, and Bosco made love to me after we showered together, which made me feel loved.

Chapter Sixteen

Bosco

I twisted the handle in my hand, pulled my hoodie over my head, and watched Corbin talk on the phone in Central Park, surrounded by security. I got word from Armani that Corbin had made an appearance at the office he was kicked out of and sued by because of the missing money. Giselle made me promise to be honest with her, and I had to be the one to tell her that her husband might possibly still be alive—even though I'd made sure to kill him.

Corbin shouted into the phone and slammed it on the ground as people watched and moved around him like he had a disease. He glanced up and peered at some small kids, people exercising, and a few joggers. I sat up on my bike and waited as he strolled to his car, piled in, and headed away. I stayed behind a few cars and moved into traffic, so as not to be spotted. Lake and a few of the Thunder bikers revved up and trailed behind us. I had to make sure we kept our profiles low and kept the media from finding us.

Corbin's car stopped at Giselle's magazine's building. My trigger finger itched, ready to pull it if he tried to go inside and start more shit. Seconds went by; his car continued, and I relaxed, following him as he led us off the major streets and down a side street. We pulled into an alleyway. I parked on the corner and watched him get out and head into the open club door. I hopped off my bike and rushed to catch the door before it closed. Lake removed his gun. I took mine out and held a finger to my lip for the security detail to not say a word. I heard talking from the office, and I burst inside with my gun, ready to kill anybody that posed a threat to my woman.

"Corbin Ford." My thoughts were fiercely concentrated on making him pay.

He jumped in fear. "What the hell are you doing here?"

"Where's Steele?"

Corbin lifted his head from the cocaine on the top of the table, and I pointed the gun at the woman on his lap.

"Darling, you might want to leave. It might get messy."

The young girl looked no older than twenty, and Corbin was in his late sixties. It turned my stomach to see him using women for his pleasures: Giselle, his ex-wife, and now the girls he probably forced himself on.

The woman raked her eyes at Corbin and back to me, got up from his lap, and ambled out of the room.

"Where's Steele?"

"Bosco, put the gun down, and we can talk." Corbin started fires, but never put them out, the coward.

I inched closer, pinning the gun to his forehead. "Tell me where Steele is, and whose business you're doing while you're drugging up with these young girls."

Corbin wiped his hand down his face. "I don't do drugs."

I smirked and motioned at the desk. "Corbin be real, right now I can see your eyes from here and the little cocaine on the top of your coat shows you're sloppy while snorting up."

"I'm not a drug addict. You sell this shit!" Corbin hissed. The years had been terrible for him.

"We're here to talk about Steele and your son."

"Bosco!" Roger shouted.

"Yeah."

"We have to go, the police have been called." Roger rushed into the office. Corbin released a breath.

Pop! I shot over his head to scare him and pushed my gun back into my holster.

"This is a warning, if I find out you helped Jason, you and your son will know torture and a slow death."

Corbin slammed his hand on top of the desk. "My son is dead because of you."

"We will talk again—and tell Steele I'm coming for him."

"He's ready," Corbin seethed, then stood and planted both hands on the back of the chair.

I walked out of the office and into the main room of the club. It was sleazy bar, with topless women in thongs, smoke filled air, and music played by a broken speaker. Dark colors surrounded the walls, and it smelled of old rust. Lake and I marched out of the club and got back on our motorcycles. Billy came over and slapped something in my hand and I peered down to see a small bag with pills and a logo that looked similar to our trucking logo on top and what looked like a phone number.

"While you were talking to Corbin, I talked with a few of the girls. One had a bag on top of the table, and she told me about how Corbin drops them off for them to relax and be more ready for the men who come over," Billy remarked.

"Son of bitch."

Billy closed his fist, stalking to his bike. "I bet it's from the first robbery."

"I thought Allen sold everything by now, but he probably had Corbin and Steele moving our product under our nose." The thrill of peeling off his skin while he was doped up on cocaine was the only thing that gave me comfort.

"We can take him out right now," Lake suggested.

"Use Corbin to find Jason if he's really alive, we can't kill him yet."

Darkness came quickly, and a cold, windy chill engulfed me. I breathed on my hands to warm up and stay awake. Finally, the alleyway door came open; Corbin got back in his car, and his security detail drove him away. A bus passed, making it harder to stay on track, but I stayed close enough to see him heading out of the city, back to the suburbs, and onto a quiet, dead-end street with a few cars parked outside. Corbin's security searched the area, and he walked up to a house and knocked.

A few minutes went by, and a woman stepped out and hugged him, then he walked inside. I climbed off the bike, slowly jogged up to the side of the house, peeked through the window, and saw a young child's room. I moved closer to the front window and saw Corbin talking with the woman as she smiled. A laughing child appeared, catching me off-guard. I moved in closer, and headlights from a car passed by from next door.

"Shit!" I hopped back to avoid being seen, left the area, and headed back to my office.

As soon as I made it to Calabresi Trucking, Giosuè rushed up to me and held out a glass of scotch. Giosuè sipped on his own drink. "Tell me what you saw."

"After dinner last night and Paul's death, something was

bugging me all night. The thoughts about Jason couldn't be true but is because the facts are adding up."

"Corbin needs to die."

I downed my scotch, then took the bottle and filled my glass again. "Not just Corbin. Steele and Jason are alive."

His brows hiked up in shock. "Jason Ford?"

I guzzled down the scotch and hit my chest after feeling the burn. "It traces back to our own people being paid off—either by Allen or Steele—to not get rid of Jasons's body."

Giosuè slammed his glass on the table. "People who worked for us?"

Armani rolled up his sleeves. "I looked into the clubs and the fight clubs. Our products are being sold in both."

"Leaving us out of the money, with more for themselves." He could feel his panic rising.

I tossed the glass against the wall. "Allen lied about Mallory sleeping with Jason because he wanted to throw her under the bus to have Giselle in a spiral." Anger and aggravation from being dupped is one thing, but hurting Giselle hyped up my emotions.

"Paul was killed by the same bullets from the shootout at the bakery," Armani mentioned.

I balled up my fist, punched the wall, spread my fingers, and ignored the pain. "Jason is alive."

Giosuè advanced on me, checking to see if my hand was broken. "What proof do you have?"

I waved him off, rifled at my desk. "Look at the picture. I'm fine."

Giosuè moved to sit down, flipping the picture back and forth in his hand. "Spook, Jason, and Corbin."

"The same man that tried to sell her," Armani commented.

"Giselle needs to know about what you've found so far," Giosuè reminded me.

"I will tell her."

Armani left his forearms rested on the back of the couch. "He's probably watched her for the past few months."

"Years. She found out an account is still open that should have been closed three years ago."

"Damn, Jason's a slimy bitch," Giosuè echoed my thoughts.

I hauled up my sleeves and clicked on my computer to look over the daily reports. "The casket was completely empty. Steele's been playing us."

Giosuè slipped a cigar, then gestured at me and Armani if we wanted one. "Using Corbin and Jason."

"I think the woman and kid I saw tonight belong to Jason."

Armani and Giosuè stared at me.

"She's going to be hurt," Giosuè said, lit his cigar, and blew out the smoke.

"Keeping this secret is hard, but I'd rather wait until we know for sure before dropping a bomb like this on her."

"Tell her before she finds out from someone else. I know Mckayla wants to do a girls' night before we fly back home."

Armani slid from the couch, then stalked to the bathroom. "Savio hates not being with his wife 24/7."

"Shit, Penelope is already trying to join in since she's had to work lately and had to cancel the shopping spree," Giosuè informed me.

"Allen is dead. Paul is dead. Armani, make the call and get the people who were there doing the cleanup to the cabins."

Armani flushed and turned on the faucet. Seconds later,

he came back to stand at the corner of my desk. "I have them sitting on ice. As soon as you're ready, we can handle it."

"Thanks, I'm ready to end all these motherfuckers."

Giosuè cocked his head and stood. "Never keep us out of the loop; we're brothers."

"I try to handle it before it comes to you. As the Don you don't need to handle my problems."

Giosuè held his hand at me, I bumped his fist. "I appreciate it, but as the Boss, you have to let me come in on some things if it ends up with my little brother getting hurt." Smoke faded in the air.

Armani, Giosuè, and I watched the camera footage from the day of the raid, then pulled up the day for the robbers four years ago. I sat back in fury of how Jason put Giselle's life in danger with his selfishness and the balls to remarry and have a family.

* * *

I dimmed the lights, waiting for Giselle to walk into the red roses that were lined up on the floor, spelling out *I love you*. I held two glasses of wine. We'd gone through a lot, and I wanted to celebrate us coming together, working out our issues, and committing to not letting anyone or anything define what we had.

The door slowly opened, and Giselle held her phone to her ear. I smiled back at her as she stood in awe. I could admit that I was not the most affectionate person; romance in general usually consisted of a quickie.

Giselle ended her call, left her bags on the floor, closed the distance between us, and took the glass out of my hand.

She coiled a hand around mine to take the wine. "What's the occasion?"

I gently nudged her purse off her shoulder, leaned in closer, pressed a kiss on her bottom lip. "I wanted to celebrate us as one."

"Is Yun here?" she moaned.

"We have the place to ourselves." I took her by the hand and walked into the dining room filled with candles and a meal for a queen.

Giselle licked her lips and gulped down the rest of the champagne, then took a hold of my glass and placed it on the table.

Giselle pushed me against the table and snatched off my shirt. "I'm hungry for something else." She slid to her knees, unbuttoned my jeans, wrapped her hand around my pole, and took me into the back of her throat. I narrowed my eyes. She'd gotten bolder and was taking what she wanted, licking under my head and massaging my balls. I was ready to take over and get my favorite dessert down my throat, so I lifted her up and planted her on top of the table, then spread her legs over my shoulders, dipped my head low, and peppered kisses along her thigh. Giselle held onto the back of my neck as I brushed my nose up and down her slit and inhaled her scent. I grasped her thigh, pushed her leg wider, and snaked my tongue around her lower lips. The heat from her naked skin sent shivers up my spine. I moved confidently, cleaning up every drop. Giselle's juices trickled down my chin as she roamed her fingers along my shoulders and back.

"Harder, *baby*," she panted.

My ears perked at her response. I stood, thrust forward, and put her left leg around my waist. The buildup had the table shaking, Giselle's head hung low, skin flustered, and she coated my dick. I forced her on her back and moved her legs up to her ears and pounded her until she screamed.

"Open your fucking eyes and see how much your pussy drains this dick." It was too intense, every sexual act before her never mattered or compared to what I have with her. Immediately flipped her over and lifted her hips to the perfect height.

I felt her body's willpower slip away.

"So full, baby...keep going."

I slapped her on the ass, watched the ripple in her ass move against my balls. "Nasty little slut, you want my dick, huh?"

"Only yours, oh Bosco!"

Gently, I moved to pull her nipple into my mouth. "My baby, my pretty lady—one day, my wife," I grunted, locking a hand on her throat.

She gasped and swept her hands up my chest.

Sweat beaded down our skin, I scooped up the glass I had and poured it down her throat and on her chest, she choked a little as I squeezed. I wish I could have killed Jason over a hundred times.

"Fuck you look sexy."

Sounds echoed in the room, banging of the dishes falling to the floor. I thrusted my tongue in her mouth to gain more of her sweet taste.

"I'm coming!"

I picked up the wine and took a gulp, then poured a little on her breast, sucked it off, and tossed it onto the floor. "Let it go, baby. You can have it all."

She released, and I fell on top of her and kissed her through her orgasm. We slowly caught our breaths, and my eyes got heavy.

* * *

Another Sunday morning came around. I was completely immersed in Giselle's life; I would do anything to keep her happy. After talking with my brothers and tasting Gigi, it was clear that the end of the Graziano and Ford families had to come sooner.

Giselle sat on top of the kitchen island and sipped her juice. I guzzled down the rest of my coffee, then hoisted the pot and refilled my mug before taking a seat and piling the pancakes, sausage, eggs, and fruit that Yun had made onto my plate. Giselle had plans to spend a little time at work, then do a girls' night. She would be preoccupied, but I had planned a dinner for the two of us to finally make it official.

"You're staring at me pretty hard, Mr. Calabresi." She grinned; her cup half-covered her sweet smile.

I placed my cup on the counter, turned to face her, took both of her hands in mine, and kissed her palm. "Before you go into work, I want to talk to you."

"Sure, what do you want to talk about?"

With a soft sigh, I planted my lips on hers. "Do you remember anything about Jason's funeral?"

"I mean it was a tough time, I was preoccupied, but my mom handled the big stuff with my sister."

"You know Paul is dead."

"Yes. Bosco, you're being very weird. What's wrong?"

"I followed Corbin yesterday."

Her energy picked up, she dropped her fork, and turned to watch me. "Corbin, did you kill him?"

"Not yet, but I will, and will that be a problem?" It didn't matter how she felt, he was going to die, but I wanted to see how she'd react.

She looked away, closing her eyes briefly. "I would like to be there. It's me who he tried to have sold like a rag doll."

"Baby you're getting worked up." I wanted to provide assurance.

Gigi rose, lifted her plate, and took it to the sink. "Sorry, keep going."

"From what I *do* know, Corbin is hiding something, and he worked with Paul and Steele to keep it hidden."

After she tossed the leftover food in the trash, she turned on the faucet to clean her plate. "Keep what hidden?" Gigi dried her hands and sat back down.

"Jason might be alive..." I blurted, cupped her arm, and pulled her seat closer.

Giselle snatched away from me and stood. "Bosco, that's not funny."

"Mi amor, I would never lie to you. I might be wrong, but you said yourself that the bank account is still open, and Jason's body is missing from the funeral home."

Giselle stumbled back in shock. "Missing?"

"Still don't know how they did it, but Corbin, Jason, and Steele along with Allen faked his death."

Gigi chuckled, waved the idea away, and removed my plate. "I think you've had too much coffee. Jason is dead."

"Then someone buried him somewhere else, because he's not at Memorial Cemetery."

She threw her hands in the air, then planted them on her hips. "But I saw the body go in the ground." Giselle looked perplexed, then bit her top lip in thought.

"You saw a casket go in the ground."

Giselle's eyes fluttered. She stumbled and held herself up by the counter, then looked back at me. "Jason's alive."

I jumped up, rushed to wrap an arm around her waist, kissed her on the forehead, and pulled her to my chest. "I know it might seem impossible, but I am learning new things after that day four years ago."

"Where's Corbin? And the bank account?"

I led her back to the chair, went to the fridge, and grabbed a bottle of water. "It's part of the confusion to throw us off from their mission."

Giselle sat back down on the stool and then looked up at my face.

I planted my hand on my chest, then raked my hand down my face. "I will protect you."

My mother was privy to some of the cartel business, but for the most part, our father made sure not to speak about major conversations that occurred whenever he came home late or handled calls that might put her in situations in which his enemies would use her against him. Little by little, the responsibility of falling in love gave me some regret, but Gigi was worth those sleepless nights.

Chapter Seventeen

Giselle

Jason's Memorial Service four years ago
I listened to the last rites and squeezed my mother's hand tight, not ready to let go. "Jason, I will miss you so much." I leaned forward and tossed a rose in the burial plot. "I know you're in a better place."

Jason's family was large and most of his cousins came from out of town and paid their respects. Corbin came up to me with his wife and she greeted me with a hug, even though I ignored the tension from our last talk of giving them grandchildren.

His mother patted my hand. "Gisele, dear if you want to come for dinner, please don't hesitate to call." She put on a fake smile.

"Thank you, Mrs. Ford. I have some of Jason's papers from his office if you want to come and pick them up."

"I will have my assistant grab them tomorrow," Corbin explained.

"Still weird to think that my heart is empty, it's hard to understand he's not going to be home."

My dad and mom helped me to the limo. I held the condolence cards in my hand and watched Corbin talk to Paul for a few minutes as the limo driver started to leave.

I made it back home to our place and watched Mom serve food to our guests. I trekked up to the bedroom, trying to feel Jason's spirit, and my memories of our life together. I lifted his shirt from the bed and stared at our wedding photos on the wall. Not long after, my stomach growled, and I left the bedroom, stood at the top of the stairs, and heard whispers from Jason's office.

"Corbin wants to handle Jason's business accounts," Mallory emphasized.

"She's his wife, Mallory; she should oversee their money," Mom muttered.

"Corbin thinks it would be too much for her and I agree, Giselle's sensitive when it comes to managing during hard times," Dad told her.

I pushed the door open, and Dad and Mom smiled at me. "What are you doing?" Everyone put on a somber look, waiting for me to crumble to my knees. I could admit that the shooting initially had me losing my mind, not eating, constantly drinking, and barely showering, but I'd come to realize that life was short, and we only had people in our lives for certain moments.

My sister closed the distance between us and wrapped her arm in mine. "Gigi, I was just coming to get you to eat."

"I was heading downstairs to eat."

"Perfect, Mom is already fussing at Aunt Catchy for being late," Mallory tittered.

* * *

Colleen clapped her hands together. "Giselle!"

I shook off the past memories. "Sorry, what?"

"You went back in time or something." Colleen laughed.

"Sorry, brain fog."

Colleen nudged me in the shoulder. I listened to the editor go over the latest stories that we should be on top of. I logged into my iPad and pretended to take notes. Ever since the conversation with Bosco at breakfast, I was still replaying his confession that Jason was alive. If I loved my job less, then I'd sneak out and join him in his search for my ex so I could put a bullet in him myself.

"So, plan those top three stories for a deadline in two days," the editor commanded. She ended the meeting, and I piled up my things, ambled back to my desk, and logged into my email to start work on my next article.

Ding!

I glanced at the alert on my computer of a new email, then chuckled at Rose Thorn inviting me to a private dinner and showcase of an upcoming dress line. I thought she'd have banned me after I slipped out of our interview, then the kidnapping.

I typed a response and finished my research on my next subject to get ready for a new story on the next big thing in fashion. Colleen walked by, holding an iced mocha for me, and I thanked her, then took a sip. My day went by so fast that I logged out as soon as I had compiled all the notes, hoping to do a bit of work from bed today. I turned to look out the window, saw rain coming down hard, and sighed in frustration. I gazed at my watch and saw that it had turned 5:30, and I had a half hour to make it to the store and home to get things set up for girls' night. It was the last time Rena and Mckayla could spend time with me before they flew home.

Colleen held up a small black umbrella. "You need one, I have this extra?"

I scrambled to gather my things and grasped the umbrella. "Thanks. I completely forgot to grab one when I left from home."

She was the coworker that every company wished they had. Colleen walked through the lobby, and we said good-bye. Keith took my umbrella as I piled in the back of the car. I leaned forward, and Keith shut my door and moved to the passenger seat.

I placed my things beside me on the seat. "Mikell, can you run me to the grocery store on the way home?"

"Yes ma'am."

I dug in and removed a napkin to dry off my bag. "Thanks." I moved to check myself out in my mirror and fix my makeup. "Can I ask you something?"

Mikell and Keith nodded their heads.

I closed the compact, slid it back in my bag, and checked my phone for any messages. "Did you know Jason was alive?"

Silence filled the car, and that told me all I needed to know.

I sighed, crossing my legs. "I won't be mad, just trying to piece it all together."

Keith turned in his seat. "We received word from Boss that he might be alive."

"Before or after the family dinner?" I investigated. I felt like Keith was the more sensible one, as we had gotten to know each other over the past few weeks.

"After." Keith groaned.

I peered through the window at the scattered raindrops along the streets. "Bosco thinks he's going to kill me."

"We won't let anything happen to you, Ms. Ford."

I smiled. "Thank you, Keith, but call me Giselle."

"Giselle," Keith says.

Mikell stopped in the parking lot of the Pine Groves Market, a few miles from the Calabresi compound. Before Keith could open the door, I let myself out and strolled in, pushing a shopping cart. My mind was on a few items from the vegetable aisle.

Keith trailed behind me, and I lifted a few trays of fruit, thinly cut meats, and cartons of ice cream.

"Oh, sorry," said a petite young woman with high cheekbones, standing with her son, after she slammed into my cart.

"You're fine. I wasn't paying attention anyway," I tittered.

"Same. Trying to keep this little one busy has my brain on overload," she explained, tickling the little boy in front of the cart.

"That cologne, it smells familiar."

She glanced down at her large shirt and shrugged. "My husband's. I threw it on and rushed out of the house." She chortled.

I laughed and reminisced how the scent was what Jason wore.

Keith moved in close, and I held my hand up to stop him.

"We're fine, Keith."

She looked at him with a confused facial expression and waved goodbye.

I shook out of my thoughts and finished my list, then

handed over the credit card that Bosco gave me and paid for the food as Keith placed everything in bags. We made it home in less than fifteen minutes, and I tossed my coat and umbrella on the counter, then started to remove groceries as Yun pulled out trays, utensils, and cups for tonight.

"Thank you, Yun for helping, I know you have a good book. What are you reading tonight?"

"A mystery series I picked up that keeps me guessing." Yun chuckled and grabbed the champagne, strawberries, and juice.

Bosco walked into the room and kissed me on the cheek. I laid the grapes on the plastic tray, turned, and linked my arms around his neck.

I grinned and plopped a strawberry in my mouth. "Hi." I put the juice back down, locked both hands around his neck, lifted off my toes, and pressed kisses along his cheek. "You're wet."

Bosco groaned, snuggled up close, and bit me lightly on the side of neck. "I can say the same for you," he whispered in my ear, brushing his nose along my cheek.

I giggled at his naughty response and moved out of his grip before we got started and ignored the entire girls' night.

"How long will you be gone tonight?"

"Not sure, I have business that can't be missed." His ambition to find the truth made me love him more.

"Does it involve Corbin and Jason?" A haze of terror fought to release itself from me, but I was too overwhelmed by the happiness we'd created.

"Business. You know I keep that to myself." From the corner of his eyes, unmistakable secrets lay in his mind.

"I had a memory of the past today."

"A memory?"

"Well, it was a flashback of the day Jason was buried,

and you're right; the casket was closed during the funeral and burial. After he was carried into the ambulance and the hospital, I never saw him again."

Bosco dragged a hand up the nape of my neck. "I will have answers soon."

"Come back home." In this moment I felt a wave of protectiveness toward him.

A dazzling smile grew on his face. "Try to not drink too much, I know the girls will be plastered, but I want to have a little alone time tonight."

"But they're going to sleep in the room with me, like a real sleepover."

The color drained from his face. "Our bed is for us and only us."

Before I let him get a word out, I nibbled on his ear. "Are you kicking your family to the floor?"

Bosco smacked me on the ass. "Hell yeah, as long as I can get this pussy." Only in these light moments could I tame the savage that lived within him.

"I will remember to tell the girls you want them to go home so you can have sex." Every nerve and cell strained toward him, melted into him.

"No, they don't need to go home, just to another room." Like second nature, he savored the clasp of my body against his.

Playfully, I slapped him on the chest. "Terrible."

He winked and left the kitchen.

I piled up the cut-up strawberries, placed them around the chocolate fondue, and picked up my napkin to clean my hands.

The front door opened and closed, and we heard loud laughter when the girls appeared in the entrance.

Rena waved her wallet in the air and craned her neck to

search around "We're here for drinks, food, and naked men. I have my money ready."

"Rena, what kind of girls' night are you expecting?"

"I was thinking we could do a little spying."

"Spying?"

Mckayla moved about the kitchen, then tossed her bag on the counter. "Rena has it in her mind that the guys are up to something, and she wants to find out where they're going."

"Bosco said they have business to handle, and he couldn't tell me what time he will be back home," I informed her, shoving the tray of snacks toward Mckayla and Penelope.

Penelope snatched a grape from the bowl and sat on top of the counter.

Rena drummed her fingers on the kitchen island, then leaned her head on my shoulder. "Giselle, you will understand once you've been in the family long enough." Rena gulped down her champagne. "The men like to hide the truth from us."

I fiddled with the nail polish to show off what I'd planned for the night. "I have all this food for girls' night."

"We can still have girls' night, I just want to find out where Sante is going. He wore all black and that means either the strip club or killing someone," Rena remarked.

I dropped my shoulders in defeat. "One hour and then we come back home."

Rena bowed her head, then pulled Mckayla to her feet. "One hour, and we need to take a car and leave the security detail home."

"Keith is not letting me leave without him." I let out an uncontrollable laugh.

Rena reached in her pocket and plucked out a small pill bottle. "Who says Keith will know we left?"

She's trying to get me killed.

Prince wagged his tail and barked.

I rubbed the top of his head, he knew what I was always thinking.

Rena laced her fingers together with mine. "Leave your little bodyguard here."

I threw my head back and crossed my heart in prayer.

Rena pushed me toward the entryway, slipping money out of her pocket. "Yun, you haven't seen anything— understand?"

Yun grinned and nodded, taking the money.

Rena showed me to the stairs. "Go change into something less obvious."

I sprinted upstairs and changed quickly, then met the girls when I got down to the garage. We piled in the car, and Rena turned on the engine. Yun stood at the door and motioned that it was clear, and we could leave now. Keith was completely knocked out in the living room from drinking water with a sleeping pill dissolved in it.

I prayed we made it back before them.

Mikell was out with Bosco, so the security detail at the gate were the only ones on duty, and they never really paid attention to me leaving, but I slumped down in the back seat anyway.

"Where are we going exactly?"

"I share a location with Sante, it shows a club they're supposed to be at tonight. Wonder what business they have to handle with loud music and girls throwing themselves around," Rena hissed.

"Calm down, killer," Penelope teased.

Rena rolled her eyes and sped through traffic.

Penelope gripped the dashboard and door handle. "Slow down Rena before you get a ticket."

"Your husband runs the city, we'll be fine." Rena pointed at Penelope.

"My husband is going to kill you and me if we have one injury, so I suggest you slow down," Penelope whined.

Thirty minutes later, Rena came up to a dark road with limited streetlights. A few people were out, drinking and yelling near the corner. Rena parked, flipped the lights off, and looked around the area to see a few men pushing themselves against some women. A few motorcycles that looked like the one Bosco rode were lined up in a row.

"Okay, listen up—we are only staying for a few minutes, then we're going back home," I explained.

Rena reached into her purse and cocked her gun. "Come on. The quicker we find out what they're doing, the better."

I covered my eyes and groaned as goosebumps prickled my skin, like a bad feeling of danger was coming. "She has a gun, Mckayla."

Everyone stepped out of the car.

"Sante is the only one that can control her attitude." Mckayla grunted and pulled me by the wrist to the side of the street.

Rena walked up to the bouncer and aimed her gun in his face.

"Oh lord, she's going to kill him," Mckayla said, a resigned sigh puffed between her lips.

Pop! Pop!

"Arghhhh!" Screaming and yelling filled the area, then the front door of the club burst open, and people pushed each other wildly to get away. Mckayla stretched her hand out to yank Rena backwards before she could get knocked down.

Mckayla shoved Rena in the direction of the car. "Let's go, we can't get caught out here."

Rena's eyes gleamed with defiance. "Wait, I want to make sure Sante is okay."

Mckayla's recognition of the situation made me feel better. Everything happened so fast, anyone could get killed by a bullet or trampled.

"They can take care of themselves, we need to get home," Mckayla responded.

"I agree with Mckayla; if they have to worry about us on top of trying to watch for bullets, then it will only make things worse."

I glanced behind me and saw Bosco with a headband across the bottom of his face. I could tell from anywhere, those dark eyes when he's on a mission. He hopped on his bike as Savio and Sante talked to each other. Relief flooded my face.

"Giselle, come on!" Penelope shouted.

I bent down, climbed in the back seat, and slammed the door.

Rena sank down low, covered her face with a coat, and turned away. "Shit! He's right there."

Sante glared at us and marched over to the car.

Rena tried to crawl over the seat, but Sante knocked on the window. "Start the car, Mckayla." Rena paused; her expression showed that she knew she was in trouble.

Mckayla rolled the window down and sighed.

Sirens from the ambulance and cops interrupted his argument, but he whispered something in her ear.

Mckayla started the car and followed Bosco away from the club.

"What did he say?"

"If we're not back at the house before him, he's going to make me choke on his dick." Rena grinned, wielding a seductive smile.

All of us burst into laughter and I shook my head. Bosco would be the first one to punish me for leaving the house, I just prayed Mckayla got us home before him.

As Mckayla left the city, rain drizzled outside the window. I was exhausted from the entire day, and I just wanted to have a simple night of relaxation, talking, and doing our nails without all the other issues.

Mckayla turned off from the freeway. "Your phone is ringing."

"Probably Bosco."

I plucked it from my pocket to see Corbin texting me.

Corbin: *I saw you tonight.*

Me: *Why are you texting me?*

Corbin: *You should have died instead of my son.*

Me: *Funny, I was thinking the same about you.*

Corbin: *Steele might have missed when he tried to sell you off, but I won't.*

Me: *Bosco is going to kill you.*

Corbin: *He's a dead man walking right along with his brothers.*

Me: *Did you help Jason steal from the Calabresi family?*

Corbin: *A bitch like you is the reason my family lost everything.*

Me*: Only reason you're alive is because Bosco can't find you.*

Corbin: *Soon we will show you and Bosco. The Grazianos will run the city.*

The car stopped, and Mckayla parked in the garage. All the men stood at the front steps with frowns on their faces.

"Stop trying to stall, come on," Savio growled, opened the door for Mckayla, pulled her into his arms, and cupped her chin, then turned her face left to right to check for any bruises.

Sante wiggled his finger at her. "Rena, come on, let's go now." Creases lined his face.

The heat of shame hit Rena's face.

I lowered my head at the scowl on Bosco's face.

He pecked me on the forehead.

"Are you hurt?" He concentrated on me, tucking his hands under his arms, while the only sound lingering in the air came from the air conditioner.

"No."

"Bosco it was my fault, I saw Sante wearing all black and had to know what was going on," Rena pleaded on my behalf before leaving us alone.

The look in Bosco's eyes said he would go along with her excuse for now, but the constant reminder of my past escape attempts whirled in his head. Without a word, he walked to the elevator and up to the bedroom.

I followed and waited near the dresser for him to speak further. I fiddled with the bottle of cologne on top of the dresser, then his watch, and I held my breath. From the corner of my eye, I saw Bosco rip off his shirt, trek to the bathroom, and turn on the shower. I stood in the middle of the bedroom with beads of sweat running down my neck. I still needed to tell him about Corbin sending me a threat. My heart was beating fast, and I knew that I had to wait to let him calm down before we had a real conversation.

"I'm not mad."

"Bosco—"

"No, you're safe, and that's all that matters, come take a shower with me."

I drew into his arms, ready to crawl into his chest. "I don't say it enough ... but thank you."

"Come shower and get clean, stressing is my job."

"Guess girls' night was a success."

He craned his neck and frowned.

I simpered and tossed my head against his chest, then stood on my toes and pecked him on the lips. We moved to the bathroom, washed up, and finished eating.

Chapter Eighteen

Bosco

After I received word that everyone made it home tonight, we showered and ate dinner, then watched a movie. I watched Giselle slip the robe off her shoulders, wink, and swish her hips as she headed to unlock the deck door. The urge to release all over her pussy was overwhelming as I stared at the sway of her hips. She gripped the rail at the edge of the bed, and I was amazed that she belonged to me. I ached to sink deep inside her. I dragged my hand down my face and rose from the bed completely naked, trailing behind her and pushing my dick against her ass. I engulfed one arm around her body, curved the other one up her neck, and kissed the side of her cheek. Passion gushed up my spine at the thought of how many years I would have to enjoy these moments. Giselle threw her head to the side and ran her palm up the back of my head. She moaned as she continued to slowly press her butt against me. Without warning, I pulled my hard-on out to find its sweet home and pushed through her barrier.

"Mmmmm...Yes," she cooed and circled her hips.

I moved a hand down to her lower lips, sucked on her earlobe, and maneuvered my hips and thrust forward.

My pretty lady spread her legs wider, whimpering lowly and forcing her nails into my hands as I bent her forward. As desire sizzled up my spine, something in my chest twisted and roared. Emotion flooded my heart at the thought of Corbin and his people coming close to her again. I moved faster as domination filled my brain.

A chill breeze eased across our bare skin, crickets chirped along with our moans of passion.

I teased her clit and she continued to meet my pumps back-to-back. An unfamiliar tenderness swept through me.

Slap!

I tapped her on the ass. "Tell me what I want to hear." A strange comfort in keeping her close to me was filled by her words.

"Bosco! Baby, fuck, wait," she begged; her head spun around to face me.

I lifted her leg and moved to the edge of the railing. She whimpered and screamed.

"Be a big girl and tell me." I craved to bury myself in her slick, warm pussy.

"I'm yours! Oh shit, fuck," she gasped as I lifted her in the air from behind and turned her around, then moved her to the chair in the corner with her ass in the air.

"Ride my dick, I know you can do it baby." I drew in a sharp breath. "You look sexy as fuck."

Gigi pushed me onto my back and lowered herself on top of my dick, planting her feet flat on the ground and pushing her hair out of her face. "Mmmmmhhh... shit."

There was a rush of need as her pussy pulsed and contracted around my dick, and her hand gripped the bottom of my chin, forcing me to stare into her eyes. The feeling of her mouth as we kissed was tender and orgasmic; the scent of her lavender body wash filled my nostrils, and her smooth, sweaty skin flushed along my body. My soul was tied to hers forever.

"Arrgggghhh, fill me up, taking your dick, the best I ever had."

"Nothing matters more than right now. Keep going."

"Like this, huh?" Gigi taunted, slowing her rocking, pecking me on the lips, and grinding on top of me.

I gripped her on both sides of her hips and pumped from the bottom up in jerky movements. A dangerous slash of desire sliced my gut.

"Baby! I love you so much Bosco, I will never let you go." She squirted for the first time ever.

I fell even more in love as she came. I cupped her by the chin and sucked on her bottom lip, then came right after her and took her hand and swiped our joined juices and stuck it in her mouth. An intimate whisper sent a medley of tingles through me.

Gigi fell on top of me, and I kissed her on top of her head as I heard her snoring.

* * *

Hours Earlier, at the Shooting

Armani hopped out of the van and stalked up to the club with his shotgun in his hand. I followed as my team went through the back door. Corbin's mistakes only made him more eager to die by my hands, and I was fed up with him hiding behind Steele. We'd confirmed that his son lied and covered up his theft with his father's help.

Rattta! Ratta!

I ducked as bullets flew over my head. I crawled to the

corner pole near the bathroom, closed my eyes, and lined up a shot that hit one of his security guards. Armani came up behind me and kicked one guy in the face before he could make it close to me.

"Take the right; he has to be here," I demanded, gesturing while the crew continued to shoot around the room. The loud banging music came to a halt; men crowded together, and some ran alongside each other out the exits. Smoke seeped in the air.

"Please, I didn't do anything," a guy who came out of the bathroom pleaded.

I shoved him toward another guard. "Take him out of here."

Armani blasted off more shots at the second camera in the corner. I marched down the employee back room and shot off the handle on one door to hear screams of women coming out.

I angled the gun at her forehead. "Where's Corbin?"

She cried. "He's down the hall."

Pop! Pop!

Armani shot them both and I shook my head, he was more ruthless than me when it came to killing women.

"The police got him."

* * *

I felt a kiss on my cheek, and it brought me out of my daze. I stopped thinking about the shooting at the club. Corbin had gotten lucky again.

Giselle leaned over the bed to snatch her phone from the nightstand, her breast smashed against my chest. "I have to show you something."

I licked my lips; they were sensitive. I brushed my hand up her thigh as she sat up.

Giselle scrolled through her cell and handed it to me. "Corbin texted me."

I looked from her back to the phone and smirked.

Gigi rested her hand on my chest. "Why are you smiling?"

"Corbin thinks he's in control. But Steele is making him look like the scapegoat."

"How so?"

"He got arrested tonight." I sighed, spitting out the words like poison.

Gigi wrapped her leg over mine. "Really? Do you think the charges will stick?" Disbelief colored her voice.

There was assurance that appeared from her body language. She clung to my body. I was sensitive to her needs and quickness to be mindful of my answers.

"I almost killed him, but he ran into the police, and he must have got a hold of someone's phone in jail."

She gave me a demanding look, not like the usual warm-hearted woman I knew. "I want him dead."

"He will be soon."

Gigi craned her neck. "And Steele?"

"He's been seen with a local pusher near one of our nearby clients' territories. I have it mapped out to take him down."

"I would have liked to see Corbin be arrested," she said, her hair tossed back and breasts smashed to my chest.

"That's the least of your worries. Come on, get some sleep."

Giselle ran a hand through my hair and leaned closer to me. "Can I come when you take out Steele?"

"Too dangerous."

"Bosco, I promise, I won't get in the way."

"Like you and the girls did tonight?" It was easy for me to put restrictions on her but if she would be hanging out with my family, then her choices were going to become more daring.

"That was Rena, I had full plans on having girls' night and then bed."

I laid a hand on her inner thigh and cupped her pussy. "We can talk about that tomorrow. I'm tired and need my medicine."

She moaned at my touch. "You're not exhausted after tonight?" She fell on top of me.

"Fuck no, I want you all the time."

A lot of control came from her power. She had no awareness of the way she'd have me out here undone if she left me.

*　*　*

Once a marksman got in place, I lined up Steele in my sight, then walked over to him and chuckled at the scowl that appeared on his face at seeing my presence in the middle of a mutual territory. A car roared through the red light, and smoke trailed behind it. Rust bloomed on the abandoned corner building. Clouds lit the sky as the sun beamed down on the back of my neck.

Byron handed off a bag of money. "Bosco, you have the package for me?"

I snapped my fingers, and one of the crew approached with a crate of produce. "We're here now. Talk your shit, Steele. I mean, you can't be seen by your uncle anymore."

Steele's sneer made me even happier. "I run the business; my uncle has no authority." He hated when I brought up his uncle taking care of his issues.

"Glad you realized so when I kill you, the funeral won't cost anything from his pocket."

"You must be hard up because your girl wanted me," he said, hoping he sounded more confident than he felt.

"My girl?"

"How's Giselle? If she misses me, let her know I can take her of her nicely." He blew a kiss at me.

I snarled, shoved him back against the wall, raised my fist, and punched him in the face. He took the hit, smirked, balled up his hand, and punched me in the side of my stomach. I hoisted his leg to trip him and kicked him in the chest. Steele crawled away, and shots passed over our heads. I rushed to hide behind the corner wall to escape, and Mikell came up behind me and gripped his pistol.

"Take out the right side and I got Steele."

I looked at the traffic as Steele ran off and I sprinted through rush hour as cars honked at us.

"Steele!"

He glanced over his shoulder and headed farther up the street. A girl on a bike rode by, and he snatched her off to block me, then made it to his car. I helped her up and sprinted into the middle of the street, shooting twice in his direction. One bullet hit the back of his window as Mikell made it to me in the car and shoved open the door. I hopped inside and barely let the door close as I leaned out the window and started shooting at the car.

"Boss, the Don is on the line."

"Push it to the rim. I want him dead."

Mikell swerved in and around the cars, buses, and cabs. A few people slowed down and got out of our way as Steele made it to his territory. I closed one eye, aimed the gun at the passenger tire, and shot as the car turned and flipped over near an embankment.

Mikell parked a few feet away, and I climbed out slowly as more cars pulled up behind us.

Giosuè jogged up to me with his shotgun.

I nodded back at him and moved in close to the smoking car, then made it to the back passenger side and saw it open. I moved around to the driver's side and saw that the soldier was slumped over dead.

Giosuè patted me on the shoulder. "Look there."

I gazed around at what had his attention and saw Steele running through the woods. Sweat dripped down my face. "He can't get back to his territory." I sprinted toward him and Steele ducked behind a tree.

I sighed and counted to three to calm my racing heart. "Come out, Steele. It's over."

"Fuck you Bosco!" Steele growled.

"We both know you're dead no matter what."

Pop! Pop!

I slumped down under cover as the bullets whizzed by my head, and I counted to myself how many shots he had left in his gun.

Ratta! Ratta!

Giosuè retaliated and shot back; one bullet hit the side of the tree, and a branch fell to the ground.

"Fuck!" Steele groaned.

"I want him *alive*," Giosuè demanded.

I jumped up and looked around to see him laid out on the ground. I held my gun up and slowly walked to his body, bent down to check his pulse, and found him with a shot in the arm.

Mikell and Keith lifted him up to carry him back to the car.

I vowed to make sure that his family would have an open casket. Steele's eyes fluttered closed as we ran through the woods to the main road. We drove to one of the Thunder bikers' empty homes that they used to sell our product.

Steele was still in and out of consciousness, and they carried his body in the house, as Gunner and Roger stood guard outside.

I removed my black gloves and watched as his body was laid on the floor. He groaned in pain.

"Prop him up."

He spit blood out on the floor. "Grazianos will retaliate if you kill me."

I grabbed the hammer from Lake's hand and stood in front of Steele. "I hope they do after all the money you and your people took from me."

Steele shook his head, put a hand on his wound, and backed up to the wall. The look of pain and anguish engulfed him as he tried to find a way out of the situation.

I jacked him up by his shirt and squeezed his neck. "Any last words before I kill you?" I spat. Saliva flew from my mouth, aimed at his head.

"Maybe I can help you." Blood dripped down his shirt.

"Help me how? Huh? You've robbed my business and made the cartel more exposed."

"I can pay you back, just give me a chance," with a muttered sob, Steele begged.

I raised the hammer in the air. "Second chances aren't my thing." Reckless anger hardened my heart. The hammer came down and knocked him to the ground. Blood splattered around the floor. Not satisfied, I hit him again and again as his body became dismembered.

"Oops, I guess I lied about him being recognizable." I tempered my anger with amusement.

"The cleanup crew is on the way now." Lake approached and took the hammer from my hands.

"A check is on its way for letting us handle him here."

We slapped hands, and I walked out of the woods, hopped back on the road, and followed my brothers to head home to see my love.

My future Donna no longer had to suffer or look over her shoulder and wait for people to try to hurt her because of me or her ex. Steele and the Graziano cartel could no longer dictate to us or have a seat at the table; I'd made sure of that. Word would spread that if anyone worked with their family, then they would no longer make money in this city.

Chapter Nineteen

Giselle

Opera music hummed through the speakers at Rose Thorn's limited, invitation-only fashion show. Models were posing on stage. Each one wore a custom gown, and Rose had named it show "The Year of the Gilded Age," with exquisite diamonds, lace, and corsets that fit each model's size and body type. Kathy, Rose's assistant, handed each of us a card that explained what we'd be seeing for the day. Catered food and gift bags were at the door. I slipped my shades over my eyes, removed my cell, and snapped pictures as the next round of models came up to the stage and posed. Penelope hugged Rena, then Mckayla, as they sat down next to her. Rose tucked the mic in her hand, then started her speech about the pieces that were being shown at the moment. Lights reflected from each gown. I admired the time it took to sew each garment, get makeup and hair done, and get the photographers and crew to work together.

The event went off without a problem, and we stood. I picked up my bag, tucked it under my arm, trekked out to the car, and climbed in the back of the Range Rover. Mikell drove me and Mckayla, while Rena and Penelope rode in the car behind us. I removed my cell and stared at the last communication from Bosco.

Bosco: *Enjoy yourself.*

Me: *I miss you.*

Bosco: *Come home.*

Me: *Soon.*

Mckayla popped a piece of bubble gum in her mouth. "Rena wants to go to lunch, her treat."

"That's fine with me. Bosco is probably going to be with the guys all day."

"Mikell, can you take us to La Mer?" Mckayla asked.

I stared out the window as the car eased through a red light, sighing at the feeling that things had calmed down. We arrived at La Mer French Restaurant within five minutes, and I felt my stomach growl as I thought about the great food I was about to eat.

Mckayla climbed from the seat. "I swear Savio is going to hate me when he gets the credit card bill." She shifted her purse to her other arm and put her hair up in a bun.

I reached for her hand. "Why?"

Mckayla turned her phone to show me she'd purchased three gowns from Rose Thorns' fashion event.

I lifted my hand to cover my mouth. "He is going to have a fit! $20,000!" I giggled, plucking my lipstick out and touching it up.

Mckayla waved Rena and Penelope over once they left the car parked behind us. My attention was drawn to something in the corner of my eye when I reached down to pick up my cell from the seat. I saw Corbin standing at the corner in conversation with the same woman I saw at the supermarket.

"Giselle, is something wrong?" Rena asked.

A car seemed to be overheating; smoke flew from the engine, while a man pulled over to the side of the road. He reached for her elbow and pushed her back to the side as they talked to get her out of his way. I turned my back to block myself from being seen and clasped Keith by the arm, moving behind the restaurant door.

I flipped my phone over and dialed Bosco's number. "Rena, take the girls back to the car. Keith, look up the street at the corner. It's Corbin." I inclined my head to the left.

Mikell walked up and guided the girls to the restaurant.

Rena tried to move around me, and I pulled her back. Keith removed his gun.

"Stay here," Mikell said.

"*Mi amor*," Bosco answered.

"Bosco, he's here," I whispered, tugging Keith out of the restaurant and going back to the car. "Follow him." All of us stood outside our cars.

Rena shot a sour look at me. "Hold up Giselle, what is going on?"

"We're at La Mer, and I see Corbin." My words felt shaky.

"All right, stay with Keith," Bosco commanded.

"No, we need to follow. I know you can track us." My stomach turned over at him getting away again.

"Giselle, damn it!" Bosco barked.

I ignored Bosco and hung up, then clicked on the video app and held up my phone to record. I got in the car and sat forward to confirm the vehicle he was driving. "Mikell, hurry—before they leave."

Corbin and the young woman pulled behind a bus and drove away from the meatpacking district. Keith's phone rang, and I heard Bosco yelling orders that he was on his way and to stay with me at all times.

"Mckayla are you good?" Savio questioned.

"Savio, we're fine. Just be careful." Mckayla locked her seatbelt and kept her speakerphone on.

"Boss, they're turning off on the main. Traffic is picking up," Keith described.

"Are they moving to the east?" Bosco probed.

"Possibly back to their home," Keith suggested.

"I've seen that girl before," I blurted out, relaxing into the seat.

Keith looked back at me. "The grocery store."

"Yes, she had a son with her, remember?" I had a vivid recollection of her and her son, and the scent she wore replayed in my mind.

"Boss, we might have a problem." Keith handed the phone to Mikell as they talked amongst themselves.

"I'm coming up on your left side," Bosco explained.

I glanced out the window and saw Bosco and a few of his men. We stopped at the light before we got on the highway.

Bosco motioned for me to roll the window down. "You all right?" He stuck a hand in the car and caressed my cheek.

The light changed. He crashed his lips to mine, and a honk of a horn from the cars behind us started up.

Bosco pecked me on the lips and narrowed his eyes. "Stay in the car, no matter what you see."

I grasped his hand and leaned in close to the window. "I will. Please be careful."

Mikell moved to the left lane and trailed behind Bosco, about four cars deep, along with six bikers driving with him to the location of Corbin.

Nervousness remained in my lower belly, slowing down the bile in my throat as we got closer. He raised a finger to gesture that we should get off, and the guys signaled back. Mikell took the right lane and slowed down as we got to the Lakewood area, a couple miles from where Bosco lived.

Mikell parked a few houses down from where Bosco stopped, then climbed off, removed his helmet, and talked to Savio.

I shoved the door open, but Giosuè slammed it back. "Stay here. It's going to get messy."

"Where's Penelope and Rena?"

"Over here," Rena yelled from the car behind.

Giosuè rushed toward their car and climbed in to grab Penelope. They kissed, and he sprinted back to Bosco. They stormed up to the house.

Awestruck by Bosco's knockdown of the door, Corbin was dragged out with the young girl and child minutes later.

I couldn't understand what he was doing with the young girl and seconds felt like hours of past pain piled up in my chest when who I thought was a dream was here in reality.

I squinted my eyes. "Jason," I whispered, cupped my forehead in confusion, and stumbled back against the side of the car. "He's really alive."

Rena's mouth dropped agape in shock. "Jason? Your deceased husband Jason?"

I balled up my fist. "My husband, that's supposed to be dead."

One of his guards tossed him in the back of the van. The girl carried her son in her arms and held him close to her chest. I jumped out of the car and slammed my hand on the door in frustration, ready to run at him, but Keith held me back. "Jason!"

"Get her in the car!" Bosco shouted.

Everyone glanced in my direction. The young girl shot a confused look at me as Jason stared back at me in shock.

* * *

I laid my head back on the side of the car, closed my eyes, and held a hand to my chest to count down and catch my breath. We followed Bosco to the cabin in the woods where he brought Allen.

Footsteps crackled across the gravel, and Rena linked her arm around my shoulder. "I won't ask if you are all right. I know if it were me, I would be ready to kill him all over again." Rena's warmth felt firm and inviting.

Penelope tittered.

Giosuè waved Penelope to him and Bosco put out a cigarette then tilted his head up at me.

I marched over to him and fell into his chest. "He's really alive." I settled into his embrace, enjoying the feeling of his arms.

Bosco kissed me on the forehead. "I can promise he's going to die, are you ready to see him?"

I pulled back. "What are you going to do about the woman and child?"

He cleared his throat, looking away from me.

"Bosco, you can't kill them." I was conscious of my statement.

He removed his arm from me and kissed me on the cheek "They've seen our faces." Softly his breath fanned my face.

Keith and Mikell stepped out of the cabin and Bosco walked in with Giosuè.

I sprinted inside before he could do what I thought he was going to do. "Bosco," I muttered.

Bosco stood there. He didn't care about being sensitive; he was in his underboss position. "I want you to leave with Keith and Mikell and go back to the house."

People moved in and out around the cabin setting up.

"The woman and kid."

"That's Jason's wife."

"His wife?" I felt the dryness in my throat.

With a stiff posture, he plucked my chin. "I found out from Corbin that he married her and had a kid." Bosco sighed.

My palms became damp, and my mouth dried out. "I want to talk to him." I heard the bitterness in my voice.

"No, best for you and the girls to go home."

"You promised I could confront him—and before you kill him, I need answers." I knocked his hands off my shoulder. "I'm owed that much."

Bosco stared into my eyes, and not a hint of understanding could be seen in his. He didn't think I should be in the same room with Jason—let alone speak to him.

"Look, that girl out there probably fell in love with the lies, same as me, and ended up having his child. They're innocent, Bosco."

"She's seen us."

"I know you can come up with something to keep her shut, pay her off or put security on them, but that kid is already losing his father. You can't take his mother."

"All right, but the minute he tries to touch you, I'm going to cut his fucking tongue out."

I stood on my tiptoes and pecked him on the lips. "I think that's fair."

Bosco twirled around, took my hand, and walked us

back into the living room. The girl's arms were tied to the chair, along with Jason's.

Aware of my surroundings, I stood in front of Bosco and directed my attention to the one person whom I'd once prayed would love me forever. "Jason, I want to know the truth." The swell of my pain was beyond tears. The tape was removed from his mouth.

Jason scanned the room with a hard glare on his face. "What are you doing with them?"

"That's your only concern?" I stopped short in dismay.

"You're my wife." Jason seethed and shifted in the chair to get loose.

His girl grumbled underneath her tape and tried to move out of the chair.

I faced her. "Did he tell you he was married and faked his death?"

"How long have you been fucking him?" Jason quipped.

I paced in front of him, hands on my hip. "You've gotten into those drugs they've been selling because how can you sit up here and question me?"

"He's a criminal. He's killed people and tortured them." Jason spat on the floor.

Bosco lunged at him. I stepped in front of Jason with my back to his front to block him from hurting Jason until I got my answers. I caressed his cheek and ran my hand down his chest. "He has no idea. You're kind—a blessing in disguise, no matter what he says. Jason is a coward." I peered at Jason.

Bosco stood behind me. "Hurry this up so I can cut out his tongue and feed it to him."

"Time to tell the truth Jason."

"The truth is that I had to work with Steele. He had

more money compared to what Calabresi was offering and he wouldn't miss anything."

"So, robbing your boss, making it seem like you were in a good place, and spending all this money was really under false pretenses?" I gave him a sidelong glance of utter disbelief.

"Baby, we can fix this, I love you and I know you still love me," Jason promised.

"Hmmmm. Urghhh." The girlfriend or I guess wife squirmed in the chair next to him.

I pointed at her. "What about your child and wife?"

Jason leered at her and back at me. "I love you, and my child can be the blessing we've always wanted. Look I know it will be hard at first, but I love you."

"Get that out of your head, I don't want you Jason, for someone so smart, you're extremely stupid." I was irritated by his words and audacity.

I turned to his girlfriend with sympathy in my heart. "Find someone who really loves you, because he's not worth the heartache. You have a child to raise." A sense of strength came to me, and my despair lessened.

She nodded.

Bosco nodded with his chin at his soldier to release her. "My people will take you to the airport, and I suggest you get on a plane and leave," Bosco ordered. "The minute we hear you are back in town, you're dead, and your son will grow up in foster care," Bosco told her.

Mikell removed the tape from her mouth, then hands, as she rubbed the pain away.

"Thank you." She cleared her throat. "Are you serious, Jason? Did you ever love us?" She scoffed at Jason.

"I love you both, we can all live together." Panic like he'd never known before welled in his throat.

"Mommy," her son cried, and Mikell brought him back into the room.

She took him out of his arms and hugged him close. "I hope you rot in hell," she snapped.

Mikell escorted her out of the cabin and they drove away.

I turned to walk away, and Jason snatched me by my hand, turning me to face him. The life we'd built was lost and no longer in focus.

Bosco cocked his gun back, shot him in the leg, and he fell to the ground.

"Arrrggghhh!" Jason screamed.

"Keith, get her out of here," Bosco demanded.

"I want you to kill him in front of me, so I can be sure it's finished." I flipped through my memories and asked myself if I ever loved him, because I had forgotten it by now.

Bosco smirked, pointed his gun at him, and shot his right leg.

Jason covered his wound. "Fuck! Wait I'm sorry, I can make it right," Jason pleaded, no longer the rich, successful, loving husband and son.

"You can't make it right. You lied to me and put me in a situation where I could have died."

Jason held both palms in prayer. "Giselle, my father forced me to help him," Jason explained.

"Well, at least you can join your father in hell for real this time." I would always bear the part of the burden that I could have played on our journey—maybe being naive, or not pushing hard enough in the beginning. Jason had impressively blinded me into choosing to see a likable person. Now, I could move on and love the right way.

Chapter Twenty

Jason

Before the Kidnapping

I knew I had a great life with Giselle, and she loved me, but underneath it all, I wanted what the Calabresi family had, and my father gave me the idea to take it from them since we handled their finances. He started an accounting business for many high-profile companies, and the Calabresi family was laid in my lap. For a little while, Ford Accounting, Inc. had brought in millions of dollars, but he made some terrible investments, and we needed to cover some of his debts. On top of that, I loved the lifestyle that came with having the Calabresi name attached to our company. After Bosco opened his trucking business, I made sure that I moved money around, so as not to look suspicious—plus, Steele had the great idea to rob them of product that we could sell to a third party and make double what they would have made from the gun sales. Drugs weren't my thing, but Steele wanted everything they had. Giselle had no clue how I paid for luxury villas when I took her on long trips. After Bosco caught onto the theft, and he thought he killed me, I paid off his team to fake my death. When I made that decision, everyone in my life—besides my father—had to be convinced that I was dead. It wasn't hard to cover my tracks, but along the way, I fell in love with Isobel, and we had a son.

I received updates about Giselle for a little while, but then it became clear I made the right decision to stay away. My father of course never liked her, and my mom was kept out of his decisions when they divorced after my death.

I parked the car, removed my gun from the glove compartment, pushed my hoodie over my head, stepped out, and looked around. Suddenly, my phone vibrated in my hand.

"Meet us in the back room."

Before I slid it back in my pocket I glanced up, marched inside, and noticed a few people sitting around drinking and talking.

I knocked softly on the door and waited for it to open. Nervousness crept up my spine as the locks turned, and I saw my father in front of me.

"Hurry, were you followed?"

"I don't think so, how are they?"

"She's scared and asking questions. I have the flight ready on the tarmac. We need to leave. Bosco knows I'm out."

"Shit. Isobel, honey."

"Jason, what is going on? Your father told me we had to come here suddenly." Isobel clung to my shirt.

I brushed a hand down her arm and kissed the top of her forehead. "I love you and Jason Jr." The admission was a lie, I only cared about my son, but he could have been with my first wife.

Isobel looked puzzled. "What is going on?"

"I will explain once we get in the air."

Isobel jerked her head in my direction. "The air? Like a plane?"

"Yes, just grab him and I will get the bags."

"Hurry, the guards are ready," my father commanded, standing at the door and glancing up the hall.

"Did you do something? Please tell me if my son is in danger," Isobel begged, then whirled around to grab our son from the couch in the employee room.

Pop! Pop!

"Damn it! They're here!" Dad yelled, slamming the door, and shifted to the camera near the desk.

I slipped the gun from my pocket.

Isobel jumped back scared. "Jason! Where did you get that gun?"

"Jason, shut her up," my father spat.

"Fuck! Isobel, calm down."

Isobel, in one forward motion, grasped my arm and shoved me back. "No, you're scaring me and our son. Tell me what is going on or I will call the police."

The door busted open to his guards with guns. "Sir, we have to go now. We're surrounded."

"All right, Jason, let's go now!" Dad exclaimed, shoving a key into his pocket.

"I promise Isobel I can explain once we get out of here." I sighed, took her by the hand, and trailed behind my father toward the back exit.

Shots went off and we ducked down in the hall and waited as more people started shooting in the club.

"They're inside; we can't hold them off," his guard informed him, then moved around the side of the wall close to the bar.

My guard raised the gun to send a shot to one of Bosco's men, but they were faster and killed him where he stood.

"Jason! Watch out," Isobel shouted, ducking low.

I whipped around at her screams and saw that one of his guards had grabbed her and pushed a gun to her head.

"Move, or she dies," Bosco's soldier demanded.

Everything happened so fast, more bullets went off as they charged into the club, I fired back to save Isobel and my son.

Suddenly, a punch to the back of my head made me stumble forward, and the gun dropped out of my hand.

Bosco's soldier kicked the gun away, snatched me up, and dragged us out of the club as sirens blasted in the air.

"Jason!"

I heard my name called, looked to the right and saw Giselle, the woman I promised to love forever.

Chapter Twenty-One

Bosco

Jason's dead body colored the floor with his blood. I was thirsty to see him take his last breath, then get Giselle back home and away from any more betrayal. I was tired of the back and forth, trying to convince Giselle that he could love her, and he'd just made some mistakes. His ultimate mistake was working with our enemies and giving Steele any type of leverage to think that he could take us down.

"Call the cleanup crew—and Keith, you're going to make sure that the bodies are destroyed."

"Corbin?"

"Bring him up here."

Keith turned to march to the back room. Corbin was escorted out with his eyes covered by the scarf and stood in front of his son's body.

"Remove it, so he can see what his choices created."

Keith loosened the blindfold, shoved Corbin forward, and forced him to sit down. Corbin blinked repeatedly to figure out where he was and what was happening.

"Jason, is that my son Jason!" Corbin shouted and bent down to check Jason's pulse.

"Get up."

Corbin picked his head up. "He needs a doctor. You killed my son!"

"Last thing on my mind is helping your son to live, this is the end of the road for you and your son."

Corbin choked back a cry. "Bastard! You all will pay for touching my family."

I chuckled.

"Family is something you have no clue about because you never tried to understand my pain! You've known Jason was alive and had a child," Giselle argued.

Corbin whipped his head in her direction. "Jason saw you as a screw only, he used you to be seen as from a wholesome family."

"I should be thanking you, because of you I found the love of my life. Bosco is more man than Jason will ever be." Giselle's stare drilled into him.

"You bitch!" Corbin seethed through gritted teeth, then charged at Giselle.

Pop!

I blew his head off his shoulders; blood and brains splattered everywhere. I cocked my head to the right and stared at both bodies.

I cupped Giselle's chin and kissed her on the lips. "Let's go home."

The door opened, and a few soldiers came in wearing all-white suits and masks. Keith directed them toward Jason and Corbin lying on the floor. Giselle slipped her hand into mine, and we walked out of the living room and back to my car. Giosuè, Armani, and the girls stood next to their vehicles.

* * *

The burning of the tires on the pavement pierced my ears. It sent a signal of sweet glory that Graziano's people were falling like chess pieces, one by one. I turned the engine off and watched the blood drain from one of Steele's soldiers, who thought he could get away with shooting at my girl. I bent down, untied him from the wheel, and marched inside Titus's undercover chop shop with my guards and brothers next to me. The startled men jumped back in shock; some tried to run, and I grinned as Armani took a crowbar and knocked them upside the head.

I slammed the butt of my gun into his head, and blood drizzled down his forehead. "Where's your boss?"

"Fuck you and the rest of the Calabresi!"

I tossed him to the ground, jogged up the two-story car shop, raised my leg, and kicked the door in. Titus scrambled to grab his gun.

"Make one move and see what happens." My voice was firm and final.

Titus held his hands up in surrender. "We can work out an arrangement."

"Too late for arrangements."

"If you kill me without the approval of the other Bosses, it will start a war."

I stopped in front of him. "You must have just met me to think I care about the other Bosses."

"Giosuè, talk to your brother," Titus hissed, and two of my soldiers stood on each side of him.

"He's the underboss, and I trust his decisions," Giosuè remarked, clapping me on the shoulder.

"We have rules!" Titus barked, trying to yank out of their hold.

"Rules? Shit I break rules all day." I felt a spark of satisfied light.

Pop!

Titus's body dropped to the ground.

My guards dragged him out of the room, and Giosuè and I walked back out and downstairs.

I waved my hand around the room. "I want the entire place burned to the ground."

"Armani, I want to find out what kind of money is being made over here—and fast," Giosuè commanded, and Armani slipped his cell out and sent a text.

A few Thunder bikers pulled up. I walked out and shook hands with Lake and Roger, then nodded at the rest.

"Word is spreading about the shooting," Lake said, then revved his engine.

"Call a meeting, put security on every block."

"Establish a presence to show the united front of the Calabresi cartel," Giosuè agreed.

"You want us to ride with you?" Lake asked.

"No, I can handle it, make sure no one tries to come and mess up what my men are doing," I directed.

Lake's crew pushed their bikes to each end of the road and set up to watch, while they cleaned out Titus's body. I climbed onto my bike and started the engine to ride back to our nightclub in the city and call for a meeting.

An hour passed and only two of the four Bosses showed up. I kept my anger at bay from going off before I pull up at their homes.

"I see we have a few people that felt today's meeting was not important to attend."

Marcheline lifted his cell and showed a picture of the crime scene from the cabin. "We find it hard to believe Bosco that you've made a move on Titus and his nephew, then took their territory." Marcheline laid it on the table. "Where does that leave us?"

"Same place you were before—with a small percentage given to you out of respect to keep the peace."

"And the Grazianos will be under Calabresi umbrellas?" Geff wondered.

Giosuè sat next to me. "They will. My brother is going to establish a presence and make it known that we will own all property and businesses."

Geff's dark eyes looked from me to Giosuè. "Their men won't answer to you."

"Then they die." I stared at him and the other Don. "Any other questions?"

Marcheline and Geff made eye contact with each other, and then looked back to me. "We are in agreement. Graziano's section is yours," Marcheline answered.

"Glad we have an understanding. Now, I can leave, and you can let the other two clowns who decided not to show that disrespect won't be tolerated." When the word got out that the Calabresi cartel took over their territory, then we could at least put people back in the area to make real money, and they wouldn't have them to feel afraid of the gangs moving in and out.

"I need to get back to Gigi."

"Right behind you." Armani trailed beside me out of the club.

* * *

A Few Weeks Later

Water trickled down my back. I rolled my head from left to right to work out the tension and kinks. I turned the faucet off, peeled a towel off the rack, dried off, picked up my robe, and came out of my bathroom. I opened the closet and picked out pants, a shirt, and boxers to get dressed. The shower steam cleared from the room as I strolled to the sound of laughter filling the house. I searched the camera screen on the wall to see my brothers and their wives.

Giselle threw her head back in laughter—even though I would have figured she'd be still upset because Jason had been killed earlier. Rena handed her a martini glass filled to the top and then sat in Sante's lap.

"Bosco, we finally figured out what Giselle sees in you," Mckayla teased.

I roped a hand around my pretty lady's waist and kissed her behind the ear. "Mckayla." I snuggled up close.

A thoughtful smile played at the corner of Mckayla's mouth. "She doesn't like when you boss her around but gives in when you fight her battles."

Rena tittered and Gigi laughed at her statement.

I stood and plunged my hands into my pants pocket. "Fight your battles?"

Gigi turned in my arms and pushed them around my neck and stared in my eyes as we swayed back and forth. "Yes, I like to see you in action."

"How are you feeling?"

Gigi leaned her head on my chest. "About?"

"Jason and Corbin being killed," I remarked.

She shrugged. "Nothing, he made his choices when he lied and left me all those years ago when he ran off to live another life."

I arched a brow in her direction. "He was your husband at one point."

"That word husband really doesn't mean anything." She tapped me on the chest. "Take you for example as my boyfriend, I consider you more of my husband because you give me love, grace, patience, and honesty even when I didn't like what you said."

"Come eat. We've been down that rabbit hole of Jason and Corbin, we can relax and enjoy our time together before we leave," Rena explained.

I ran hands up to Gigi's shoulders and massaged the kinks out of her shoulders, while Rena and Sante went back and forth.

"Shush... look, guys." Mckayla grabbed the remote and turned the volume up.

"Breaking news: We have confirmation that the body of the notorious Steele Graziano has been recovered, along with DNA testing of Corbin Ford. Some may remember that his son Jason Ford was killed four years ago," the news reporter explained.

Gigi laid her head on my shoulder. "I can bury the past behind me and truly move on."

"What will happen to Ford's estate? I know his ex-wife has remarried," Mckayla mentioned.

Rena took a gulp of her drink. "Gigi if you had proof Jason was still alive, you could have used that money."

She looked up at me, and I saw in her eyes that she wanted me to contact the woman he had a child with. "Jason's money means nothing to me anymore, but I know who *could* use the money."

I let them leave the country and put them on a flight to Seattle with some of my guards keeping an eye on them to make sure she never talked again.

Giselle rose from the chair. "Do you think it's possible?"

"If that's what you want."

"For his son, that's who will suffer the most in the end." The glow from her smile softened her features.

I plucked a cup from the cupboard and poured some coffee. "I can put in some calls and see."

Rena stretched her arms wide for a hug, then embraced Giselle. "We are heading back to Chicago. You should come and meet the family, Gigi."

"I don't know, work is going to get even busier." Giselle sighed.

"Actually, that sounds like a good idea, a trip with just the two of us."

* * *

I never intended to fall for a woman like her and see the sun shining down on her beautiful face as she ran back from the ocean in her red bikini. She was smiling bright and wide, with no anger but only love in her heart.

Giselle plopped down in front of me on the cabana chair and picked up the towel and dried her hair. "The water is so good. It's relaxing."

I pushed her hair out of her face. "Are you having fun?"

"I am. Thank you for treating me to a quick getaway before we have to get back to our real lives." Giselle planted her towel on her lap.

"Anything for you."

"Rena sent me photos from the family and said to come out to visit soon, your sister wants to meet me."

"My sister stays in my business."

Giselle laughed. "You have a big family. I would love to meet her and see how you are with her."

"Protective, same with you."

Giselle tossed her cell on the towel, then cupped both sides of my face. "I love you."

"I love you more and more every day, gorgeous."

Epilogue

Bosco

A huge weight lifted off my shoulders when I spotted Giselle laughing with her family. Tonight's party was to celebrate her latest story about the women she'd encountered when she was taken by Corbin and Steele. Even though she was not with them for long, it had left a lasting impression. Aaron and I came to an agreement over the past few months and agreed to be cordial, but we weren't best friends. Maura, on the other hand, was my biggest support. Mallory still hated me, and the feeling was mutual. I offered to help her get a business off the ground, and that made things a little calmer between us, but I avoided being around her for the most part. My entire family and Giselle's came out for the event. She wore a formfitting gold-and-silver gown. The diamonds I gifted her with last week were displayed on her hand and earlobes. She ambled to me with her sister beside her, then slid a hand up the back of my neck.

"Having a good time, gorgeous?"

"I am, thank you for coming tonight. I knew these things

aren't your favorite being in the public spotlight." Giselle's plump breasts looked remarkable in her dress.

I pecked her on the cheek and stretched a hand around her waist. "I like seeing your name in lights."

Giselle leaned her head on my shoulder.

Rena strolled next to us and bit into an appetizer. "Bosco, tell us the truth: Are you ready to settle down?"

"Sante know you're over here."

Rena waved off my comment. "My husband understands I need to get out more." Dark red-gold hair fell into her eyes.

"Probably getting on his nerves."

Giselle slapped me on the shoulder and Rena flipped me off.

"Excuse me, ladies, I need to speak to Giselle alone." I clasped my hand on hers, walked out of the room, down the museum hallway, into an office, and shut the door. I pushed Gigi against the wall and slipped my tongue into her mouth, hugging her close. "Let's skip out," I suggested.

Gigi reached for my hand and moved it to her inner thigh. "I have a surprise for you." Gigi smiled, and her seductive young body fell against my chest.

"You're not wearing panties?"

Gigi opened her purse and removed a key.

I held a perplexed stare. "A key?"

Her finger traced along my lip. "Yes, I know you love riding bikes, and I thought, 'What would be a great present for Bosco that he could always remember me by?'"

"What did you buy?" Luxury was a normal thing in my world, but I never wanted her to spend her own money on me.

"You bought me a bike, and you've been teaching me how to ride, so I figured why not give him an entire building with the most classic bikes since I knew your brother has experience in classic cars."

I pressed every inch of my body against hers. "Seriously? You got me an entire lot of bikes?"

"Yep. Come on, Mikell is waiting on us." When she bent her head, I met her halfway.

"What about your party?" The impulse to rip her dress off and fuck her, no matter if her family stood outside the door, was strong.

"The only party that matters is the one with you."

I leaned forward, smashed our lips together, pinched her nipple through her gown, and ran a hand up her throat.

"When I get you home..." Excitement mounted within.

"Fuck me like you love me."

I groaned, pecked her on the lips, and left the room. We slipped out to our awaiting car. Mikell started to open it for Giselle, and I stopped him, telling him to go ahead and start the car, then I helped her into the back.

Giselle slid over, and I linked our hands together and lifted hers to kiss the back of her palm. She rubbed her hand against my chest, crushed her lips against mine, and bit my bottom lip gently. As soon as Mikell arrived at our designation, I angled my head out the window in awe at the building that was a few blocks from my trucking company.

I climbed over the seat and stepped out. Giselle hugged herself close to me and grinned. "When did you have time to set up the building?" I climbed over the seat and stepped out.

Giselle grinned.

The air vibrated around me, and I felt like a teenager again.

Giosuè and Armani walked out of the building, smirking. My brothers were locked in for life with Giselle and loved her like a sister.

I slapped hands with them. "You two knew she did this for me?" Before her, life was just a predictable forecast of work and random women.

Giosuè clapped me on the shoulder. "We were sworn to secrecy."

Penelope bolted toward Giselle, and I watched them hug, blissfully happy.

"Penelope, I thought we were friends."

"Bosco you are hard to keep a secret from, but I knew Giselle wanted to do something special for you," Penelope exclaimed.

Giselle motioned to the door. "Come on, let's go in and check it out."

I stuck the key in, smelled the fresh paint, and watched the lights pop on to a large, spacious floor of different motor-cycles lined up against each other. It was a one-story building labeled *Calabresi Cycles*.

Our closest family stuck around with me as I went through each bike, checked out the garage, and looked over the specs. The amount of inventory was around six million dollars. The Calabresi cartel labeled Giselle as an enemy, but her kindness, sweet ability, and not being afraid of me made me not fear what she was.

The next day, I helped Giselle climb onto the back of my bike and hold on tight as I pulled out of the gates. The wind blew, the sun shined, and the low humming of the bike filled my ears. I had my favorite girl with me. These past few months showed me what life really meant, and what mattered more than money. Our destination appeared closer as I sped up to the cabin that my family owned outside the city. Mikell and Keith followed in the car behind us and parked near the secondary employee home on the property that Giosuè had expanded after buying more land. I'd added a basketball court, plus a spa and theater inside. Gigi tried to offer to take in some of the groceries, and I nudged her to go sit down and relax. We walked into the house and saw the welcome sign that Giosuè had jokingly put up. I snatched it down, and Giselle laughed, bumping me on the shoulder.

Giselle clasped her hand in mine and dragged me through the house. "Come on, let's go start lunch, and then we can go out to the lake and watch the stars tonight."

"There are s few stars I want you to see, but we don't have to wait for it to be nighttime." I lifted Gigi in my arms, inhaled her familiar scent and walked to the kitchen with a big smile on my face.

Armani: A Dark Mafia, Enemies-to-Lovers Billionaire Romance

A one-night stand with a mafia billionaire turns deadly when Kristina learns that he's her father's greatest rival.

Kristina was ready to escape her family and the illusive family business. When she succumbs to a night of passion with a handsome stranger, she never imagined the trail of events that would follow. Especially when she learns that their families are rivals and Armani begins to blackmail her to hurt her family.

Armani Calabresi is determined to get revenge for his father's death. As the youngest of three brothers, he brings to light a longstanding feud between rivaling families that many would rather keep under wraps. He knew that sleeping with Kristina would hit her father where it would hurt the most; he just didn't expect to sleep with her again.

They might have mistaken each other for lovers, but now it's clear they're enemies. Whose family will win the war that has just begun? Or will they destroy each other instead?

Acknowledgments

I want to dedicate this to my team that helps me behind the scenes, from my editors, test readers, graphic designers, and the list goes on. I truly appreciate each of you for keeping me on my toes.

About the Author

L.K. Ryan is an author of Romantic Suspense, Dark Romance, and Contemporary Novels. Join my newsletter and sign up for the latest news and updates on my books and releases: